MW00716576

OLDER THAN RAVENS

OLDER
THAN RAVENS

Douglas Reimer

TURNSTONE PRESS

Copyright © 1989 Douglas Reimer

Turnstone Press gratefully acknowledges the assistance of the Manitoba Arts Council and the Canada Council.

Turnstone Press
607-100 Arthur Street
Winnipeg, Manitoba
Canada   R3B 1H3

Cover illustration by Steve Gouthro, oil on panel

This book was printed by Hignell Printing Limited for Turnstone Press.

Printed and bound in Canada

"A Picture of Jesus" previously appeared in *Rainbow Papers* and "The Cable Slider" appeared in *Dateline: Arts*.

Canadian Cataloguing in Publication Data

Reimer, L. Douglas (Leigh Douglas), 1947-
Older than ravens

ISBN: 0-88801-137-7

I. Title.

PS8585.E564O5 1989   C813/.54   C89-098144-2
PR9199.3.R456O5 1989

To Martha and Jeff

Thank you David, Dennis,
Marilyn and Pat for your help.

Contents

Mary's Corner / 1

Going Home / 13

Cream and Whey / 25

A Picture of Jesus / 37

Baptism / 45

The Ice Patch Field / 49

Vigil / 59

A Few Green Branches in Spring / 63

Red and White / 71

The Retarded Dycks / 85

Hell's Gate Canyon / 97

The October Rebellion / 111

Crazy Creek / 121

Fishing Men / 137

The Cable Slider / 145

Taking It Easy / 151

MARY'S CORNER

I hit the brakes at Mary's Corner and Old Henry fish-tailed, spraying gravel from both shoulders into the allowances. The Zippo cigarette lighter spilt off the avocado Export package and rattled down the length of the dusty metal dashboard. I was running ahead of the storm. Richard sat on the porch of their old farmhouse and from where he was he had seen me coming. He looked calm, as if such a commotion were common. His eyes were peaceful as the blue Pembina Hills that swam on the horizon like smoke, hills through which at this moment the Pembina was sliding southeast for a rendezvous with the Red in the flat country below Neche.

Before the car stopped, I sprang into the swirling dust. The radio in the car belted out Mick Jagger's "Satisfaction." My legs felt as lifeless as Ederle's, flutter-kicking those last yards to some English beach and groping for the solid gravel underneath. I've done it! I've actually crossed the English

Channel, she must have thought. And I was thinking, I need to sit down on the porch beside Richard even though he's waiting for me to explain and I should be standing when I start.

I had always entered his yard respectfully except for the time I saw the green light up over Harder's big elm. I'd sneaked out the basement window after my eleven o'clock curfew and was walking the half mile through the village to Richard's when the sky went green. I saw a green piano inside the Harder living-room window; two green cows behind their house tethered by the deeper grass in the railway ditch, looking upwards; a half mile of incandescent green barbed wire; and cumulous clouds with green silver linings that might have been purses. Everything had the quality of light shining through a green summer skirt. When I told Richard, my teeth did what those *True Confessions* stories would call chattering, as if I'd been trying out Buffalo Creek too early in the season. But neither of us chose to write a poem about it, so I suppose it didn't mean as much to us as love or Keats or cornstalks rustling under the moon.

My mother dabbled in poetry when she was a girl, but besides Richard none of my friends or their brothers or fathers ever gave it a shot. Why Richard and I kept at it is a mystery to me. It started in grade eight under Siemens who handed back my first-ever verses with a smile. He never smiled, at least not at me. I remember two things about that poem besides the praise: some lines concerning a grove of poplars; and my fiddling with its metre. At first it was:

> A Grove of ancient poplars stood
> By a running brook.

which I made:

A grove of ancient poplars
      stood
By a clear run
      ning brook

And the red underneath: "Regier, I see that you might just have some talent after all." I should have made it "stone-swimming brook," I have thought since. The hiss of current in that, and the "stone" to make up for the romanticism. But that's how we tend to shape the past. We itch to make life easier than it was, or more profound.

The two of us specialized in love poems and it was an obsession on and off for the next five years. An escape, I guess, from finding women and actually doing things with them; or maybe more a substitute, a keeping the machinery oiled and ready if ever an unsolicited opportunity arose. Getting lucky, we called it.

When my mother was a teenager, in the heartland of farming Mennonites south of Winnipeg near the American border, where no one seemed to get an education past grade eight, only girls and women wrote verses. Strictly entertainment. Standard Emmeline Grangerford. It's astounding to think about that time. Lawrence would soon be writing "The Ship of Death," Yeats had just finished "Leda and the Swan" and John Glassco was busy on Montparnasse hobnobbing with Callaghan, Stein and Hemingway and writing his memoirs. In 1928, Eileen Cornelson wrote something about Johnny Shaftoe in my mother's cobalt Signet pocket autograph book with the multicoloured pastel pages, and my mother added underneath:

If Johnny lived over the ocean,
If Johnny lived over the sea,
If Johnny lived over the ocean
What a good swimmer Susan would be.

This sounds like a schoolgirl's skipping rhyme or something out of Mother Goose. The sort of thing you'd expect from a manure-slinger's daughter. But it's connected in its own way with that Empyrean of culture out there a continent and an ocean away. No question, my mother was oblivious to the Bloomsbury Group, or Montparnasse, or even Broadway, the cauldron of pop art that was separated from Baergfeld by a different sort of ocean altogether. Oblivious, but not unaffected. Her lyrics are startlingly close to those of a popular turn-of-the-century Broadway tune that begins,

> Reuben, Reuben, I've been thinking,
> What a grand world this would be,
> If the men were all transported
> Far beyond the Northern Sea

and ends with Rachel swimming after Reuben over the sea.

How odd. My mother informed in some oblique way by the New York stage! Maybe she heard the song at a dance she told me once she had sneaked out to attend. It's tempting to imagine my father as Reuben, offering to share with his Rachel every paycheque of his life. Rachel foolishly refuses, he transports himself across the salty brine—a stop first to take in the giddy lights of Broadway, then bohemian talk and food in the bistros of, say, Montmartre, and French literature at the Sorbonne—and remorseful, lovesick Rachel swims the ocean to claim her one true love. Susan Rachel Regier, love's swimmer.

There were kids my age in the W.C. Miller Collegiate who were bright. Born bright. Terrence Wiens (Trotter), a red-headed kid with bad breath, scored nineties in chemistry and managed at least eighties in everything else. Alden Teichrob, who moved to Venezuela after grade ten with his missionary parents, had ten thousand volumes of science fiction stacked in his attic rooms. He collected his hundred percent on any essay or composition he wrote and finished them in less time than it took me to come up with an outline. James Dyck, son of F.O. Dyck, who ran a printing press that later grew into an international publishing company, won both the Pembina and the Manitoba provincial debating competitions two years running. Talk, this guy could talk. But not one of them, and no other male that I remember, ever mentioned poetry outside the English class. Not once. We didn't know about power then, about the thrust of language. When I finally did write for a woman it was like tossing water into sulphuric acid, though I didn't have a clue about follow-through. Maybe I wasn't dumb enough.

I'd been standing too long and decided I'd better get started. I've never liked to keep people waiting. "Richard, I just . . . It's so stupid. This is between you and me, okay?"

Richard shrugged his shoulders. "Sure, why not?" He was thin, aesthetic looking, seventeen years old, with hair the colour of coal and blueberry eyes. A perfect lady's man if he'd have believed in his looks. I sat down on the porch beside him, hunched forward so I could talk without having to look at his face. My hands hugged my elbows and my forearms pressed in as if I had swimmer's cramps.

"I was just at Mae's. . . ."

Mae, you've got to know more about Mae. Mae was the only girl I'd ever spent any time with. We'd been going together on and off Sundays in the gang I kicked around with for a few years. The guys took turns borrowing their fathers' cars. A boy with 400/20 vision, a twenty-three-inch waist, ankles too skinny to keep up socks, size twelve feet and a stammer that forces even sympathetic people to tell him to get on with it, appreciates any living thing that will tolerate him. So I had stuck to Mae even though she didn't, until this event, give off enough warmth to heat the inside of an eiderdown.

"And we were just, you know, fooling around a bit," I said, wanting to talk about it but worried, even with an old friend like Richard. Knowing the falls were ahead, wondering how close I should get. Still, it felt good for a change, him listening to me about making it with a girl.

"After a while I put my hand on her breast, you know, from outside her dress," I said. Richard was watching my lips. "She's never let me do that before! I was even moving my other hand up her calf, slowly, so that maybe this time she'd let me go past her knees, and then . . .

"Richard, I couldn't believe it! Maybe I shouldn't be telling you this, but she spread her legs a bit so I could feel up higher. Right up her bare legs. I was trembling so hard I couldn't stop!"

"No kidding," Richard said. I couldn't tell if he believed me, something came into his eyes, but he leaned in a bit. "No kidding."

"Yeah, yeah, my arms and my knees were shaking like they'd come apart! We're really kissing now and my arm is pushing her skirt up and I can see most of her bare legs out of the corner of my eyes." And then he starts to smile, Rich, and I can't stop. "I inch my hand up slowly, slowly, 'cause I don't want to scare her and make her clamp shut, like, and suddenly I touch her girdle!"

"Her girdle! Crykes, Peter, a girdle?"

"Yeah, she's wearing one of these half girdles, stiff and nylony, you know?"

"Aw, come on."

"No kidding, Rich. I have no idea what comes over me. All of a sudden, I just jump up and tear out of there—don't say a word or look back or anything—just dive into Old Henry and take off! I mean, I take off! Gravel flying in reverse off the driveway. Sixty down Main!" Rich smiling. "Think I'm crazy, or what? Should I of stayed? Would you?"

Richard had nodded a bit while I was talking, but now he

hesitated. It must have been my earnestness, I sound so sincere when I'm scared like that. I'm thinking of the time I told my parents about seeing my sister in the back seat of somebody's car with Gary Giesbrecht. I wanted to make it half funny but I seized up inside and sounded like I was talking to Reverend Brunk in the back of the tent after a revival meeting.

Rich took some Player's cigarette tobacco out of his shirt pocket before answering. "Well, who knows, but why didn't you at least stay a bit longer?" he said as if he would rather not give me advice. And then his voice got sharp. Almost angry. "You didn't have to go all the way, you know. At least find out how she's put together. Why'd you take off anyway, Peter?" Fierce grey light, reflecting somewhere, burned my eyes. The barn's grey hip roof heaved with the thrust of a standing wave.

"I don't know, for sure. I guess I was scared or something. I just couldn't stay, okay?" I tucked my arm in closer to my stomach.

"I wouldn't have left," Richard drawled, imitating Palladin or the Rifleman.

"No?" I was worried that my voice sounded too surprised. I didn't want to be taken for a fool.

"Nope."

"You and Harold!" I couldn't help throwing that one at him. Harold was no friend of ours.

"Well, not quite." Richard looked hurt, ready to change the subject. I had to say something to bring us back together again.

"It wasn't the way we thought it would be. At least not for me. Not like Wetzel and Betsy. Not like 'Bold lover, never, never canst thou kiss.' "

"But it's all part of it in a way," Richard said, his lips not pouting now.

"Yeah, I guess so. Sometimes I wish I was more like Harold." Richard laughed, and leaned into my shoulder.

Harold was a year or two older. After grade nine, he'd left Altwelt to work for the Bilt Rite Sheet Metal Co. in Winnipeg, eventually got laid off, and was now back home farming with his father. He had a utilitarian attitude toward women, one which he seemed to have been born with and which we could only imagine. He carried a record sheet in his trucker's wallet that he'd pull out dramatically, secretively, for special boys to see.

"Hey! Hey! Get your paws off. Don't touch my girlfriends with your lily-white fingers," he'd say, wiping germs from the paper. The sheet was divided into columns with anatomical headings under which he'd checked off what he'd done with Betty Kroeker or Rita Remple or Jane Sawatsky on such and such a night. Some names had three or four check marks under one date.

The Harold incident that startled me most, the only one concerning him that I couldn't forget, outside of the time he set up his friend, Werner Franz, for a beating, had happened only a week or two before.

"I'm starting to hang around the country schools at recess and lunch hour," he'd said, leaning away from me, smug, older. "I can always get some grade eighter into the car to feel up, any time I wanna. Yesterday, in Schoenwiese at recess I even had time to screw Eileen Schantz."

"Come on," I said, really surprised now.

"Yeah, yeah, I did! Okay, so I warmed her up for it the day before. You probably don't know her, but ooh wheee!"

"You wouldn't have had time," I said, laughing, pretending to be only slightly interested, sipping a Black Label from the six-pack we'd picked up from where he'd stashed it in the granary a few miles out of the village.

"Sure I did," Harold said. "It only took ten minutes." The

slug he gave my shoulder hurt like hell, but I didn't let on. He leered at me, then guzzled his beer and let out a happy belch.

"Actually, you blew your chance again," Richard was saying. "Just like last year with Flat Pat. You said that if you got another chance you'd, you know, do something with it. You have to make hay while the sun shines, Regier! You can't go peeking in windows forever."

This was what had happened at the Dairy Queen the previous spring. We were loafing in his canary yellow '51 Ford flathead which he'd backed in so that its trunk nestled under the overhanging branches of the trees that lined the parking lot. The new paint job at Corny's Auto Body had cost him a summer's savings and there in the yellow wash of the after-rain street it glistened like the glossiest nail polish. We were too poor to buy ice cream and just watched others approaching and lining up at the window. The drooping willow leaves rustled like silk on the trunk and roof and sprinkled the windshield with occasional waves of mist.

"Look!" Richard's whisper was fierce and reverent. "Flat Pat and Mary Jane Martins! I'm going over there to talk to them. Maybe they'll come over. Wait here."

He sauntered toward them and I waited. They won't come, I thought, they won't come. What if they do? What will we do? I smell sweaty. I know one thing, I'd like Mary Jane Martins to sit with me. Press against me with those faded blue jeans. Feel her heart beating against my arm like the sea washing up on the beach in the windless silence, hours after the storm. I would wrap my arms around her slenderness, and feel her push and push like a drowning swimmer. Mary Jane looks like my picture of Annette Funicello, I thought. All the other guys carried safes, they said. I carried that picture in my wallet so long it was crumpled and faded almost beyond recognition.

Richard talked to them for a minute. They talked to each

other without looking at him. He came back alone. We waited for fifteen minutes and then oh oh they ambled in our direction. There they were and they stood ten feet away talking to him. And then there they were, in. Slow glances behind them, and they climbed into the back seat. Flat Pat had dusty, hay-coloured hair that was teased back and stiff. Mary Jane's black curls looked like wet paint. Their perfume filled the car.

We stopped at my house to pick up my guitar and without asking the girls where we should go we headed to Buffalo Bush. The night was dark. Frogs by the thousand in the starlit bulrushes at the edge of the creek. Beaten to the music by a bunch of frogs. Almost immediately, Richard and Mary Jane disappeared into the bush and there I was, alone with Flat Pat. What now? The attention of the universe seemed fixed on my hands, the guitar fixed in them. I said we should go outside, felt my way to the front of the car and sat down on the hood. Flat Pat followed after a minute or two and climbed up beside me.

I began to sing, too quiet and intense as always. Nobody ever likes that. John Sebastian's "Summertime." I thought of putting my arm around her waist and felt that she might even want me to. But I couldn't do that right away. She'd probably feel I was too aggressive. The Animals' "House of the Rising Sun." Maybe she'd think I was a good singer, say something nice. Then I could move closer and start by holding her hand. If she liked it I could try something more. But she didn't talk and she didn't look at me. She crossed her legs, bare, white under her knee-length skirt, and studied her nails in the light that shone from inside the car. Dylan's "Saint Augustine."

I was still singing when Richard and Mary Jane waded out of the shadows. They weren't walking close together now. No one spoke. He started the engine and we drove the girls back to town. A few times they whispered to each other. When we approached town, they told us they wanted to be dropped off on Main Street at the Mayflower Inn.

"Why didn't you try something?" Richard asked.

"I don't know. She didn't seem to want me to," I said. My knees hurt. I had them propped up against the metal dashboard because Richard had the seat pulled too far forward for my legs.

"Come on, sure she did. She's gone out with hundreds of guys. She's been through the mill. Was just waiting for you. You should have left your guitar at home, you know." He looked at me as if I were an idiot, and humphed.

"Yeah, I know. Jeez, I'm stupid. What about you? Any luck?" I knew I sounded too eager.

"She's got a great body! Nice small breasts about like apples," Richard said. He'd had his fun. He didn't mind sharing this much.

"Come on! Really? You didn't really get to feel them?" I asked, my throat tight and dry as if I were chewing chicken feathers.

"Sure," he said, caressing the wave of his hair with a thin hand. I felt sick. Why didn't any of that ever fall in my lap?

"She didn't mind?" I asked timidly after a courteous pause.

"Are you crazy? She loved it," Richard said. His odd, high laugh seemed to get away on him.

We sat on his porch for a short while longer, and then walked out to the pond behind the red barn that was peeling and in need of a fresh coat. As we approached the water, a frog at the edge sank lazily out of sight, changing colours as it descended. Kick, kick, kick. Green, to yellow, then to the colour of the water itself.

I tried to explain but nothing I said was right. "I was just tired of going out with her, I guess. If I got involved now I was making a commitment and the way things have been going in the last year, you know."

Richard took his old corncob out of the pocket of the leather cowboy vest he'd inherited from his grandfather and blew into it and then tilted it to peer down the raspberry stem. He didn't answer. The electrical fence transformer in the barn behind us clicked on and chunked off, clicked and chunked.

"Done any more work on 'Ode to Morning'? I still have to find an ending for my 'Time' one," I said, anxious about the lag in our conversation.

"Nah. Haven't got around to it for a while," he finally said, his mouth taut, as if he hardly thought it worth giving even that much. He wasn't interested anymore, and I wasn't either now. As we walked back to the house neither of us spoke.

I drove slowly going home and I didn't turn on the radio. I wanted quiet. Caution, that's what I need more of, I thought. Don't be reckless. This is Mom's special car that Dad bought for her specially. Don't wreck it for her. Don't be rough on it.

So I cruised meekly around Mary's Corner, puttered the length of the village road in second gear, and eased Old Henry's nose into the driveway and toward its parking space of crushed rock beside the garage, off the cemented section. I could hear every beat and click of the engine and it sounded smooth and true. Strong as a swimmer in the first leg of the crossing. If I took good care of her, she would run like this forever. Never decay, never need any parts, never need a tune-up. I was pretty sure she would last forever. I turned off the key and sat there looking at the metal dashboard. The blue fuel needle, teetering a second where it had been on half full, sank behind the dusty glass like a catfish in the Red and stopped finally a quarter inch below the E that stood for empty.

GOING HOME

THE CHASE

Charles Hildebrandt ran down the railway tracks towards Altwelt. He was being chased by three or four men. They were a good three hundred yards back. He wasn't used to running. Each foot jerked forward as if it had stepped in glue, and his arms hung down too straight and pumped back and forth out of time with his steps. Brown and green grasshoppers clicked and sizzled up from underneath his feet. Some stuck to his pantlegs, some settled on the hot steel tracks, and some disappeared in the long green grass on each side. Cinders sprayed around his black shoes. They'd been polished often and didn't keep a good shine. The creases in the front leather uppers were too deep for the shining rag to reach. It was hard running on the ties. They weren't spaced right and many of them had rotten edges. They wavered like mirages in his eyes fixed at his feet.

The revolver in his jacket pocket was useless because the men behind him had a rifle. In the bright sun, light glinted from its barrel. They called something to him that reached him indistinctly. The only other sounds he noticed were the crunching and sliding of his shoes on the cinders and ties and the hysterical crescendo of a meadowlark sitting on a post of the barbed-wire fence that separated the pasture on his left from the railway ditch. He tripped, caught himself before he fell. When he looked up he saw that he'd only come as far as Groening's. Not even half-way to town, he thought. Useless. This running was useless. He'd never make it. Only this far, only a quarter mile, and already his lungs burned as if they'd been punctured. Anyway, it didn't matter anymore.

The sun blasted the back of his hair and the shoulders of his grey suit jacket. The glare off the rails burnt his eyes. The two tracks ran on straight into town, into the Ogilvie elevator painted a calendar orange and yellow, the yellow part an earlier coat that showed through where the orange was beginning to peel. Only half-way there, he thought. Half-way to the cool green trees. Enns, or Neustaedter, or Wiebe, or all of them would be in Harry Wong's now. They were always there in the early afternoon. Inside the door there'd be laughter and the hum of voices.

Enns was at Wong's talking to Neustaedter. They were standing outside the screen door, looking at Enns's new sorrel mare tied to the hitching post outside. Neustaedter pointed at the animal with the cigarette he'd just rolled. Thiessen figured he'd done okay in this deal, he said, laughing, but he might have a hard time convincing Andres at the elevator that the wheat he'd got for the horse was #2 grade. Two pots of coffee brewed on the heating element against the window where they could be seen by passers-by. Cherry, apple and raisin pie reflected from the mirror that covered the back of the glass case above the cash register. The sun shone warm and yellow through the high mainstreet window and stunned flies buzzed on the sill. A half-moon of letters on the glass facing the street said "Harry Wong's Diner" backwards.

Tina, the waitress, stepped from one booth to the next. She wore a white lacy blouse open at the throat. Her breasts bulged and shook as she reached this way and that to wipe the counter and tables. She'd keep her eyes on the table to give the customer a chance to peek down her blouse at them for a second or two as she buffed the chrome serviette dispenser or rearranged the ashtray beside the chrome fence that corralled the glass salt and pepper shakers. She leaned over the edge of a table, lunging at it with quick, impatient swipes. Through the screen door Enns watched her buttocks strain against her skirt.

Only half-way there, Charles thought. Who could have guessed it'd end like this? On the railway tracks. And not even a year out! He'd been so sure that he was well. That they'd read him wrong all along. Last March when he'd first heard that he was being released from the Rehabilitation Centre, he'd written to John Pankratz in Altwelt, Manitoba. It's just a sanatorium, he'd said. The doctor tells me that my nerves have steadied themselves, for which I praise God, and that what I needed all along was a chance for a rest. I'm looking forward, however, Lord willing, to stepping back into my accustomed harness and resuming my place as a responsible citizen doing the sort of work which the Lord meant me to be engaged in. I've learned a great deal here in the United States of America which will stand me in good stead. I'm sure that my experiences here in Minnesota have broadened my outlook and have prepared me to be a better instructor of children than could have been possible had I remained in Manitoba. And the Lord knows that our children are frequently inadequately instructed. They are bright young minds whose imaginations would be strangled by a teacher who himself lacks imagination and moral wisdom. There are so many experiences that I would like very much to share with you and I hope soon to be able to do so if you can arrange for me to teach in the elementary school in Altwelt.

Charles had good reason to turn to Pankratz. If Charles had any sort of a connection anywhere, it was him. He could be counted on to get things done. Plus, Charles knew the Pankratzes personally. They'd invited him to Sunday dinner a few times during the summer that he'd worked for the CNR there. Actually, the invitations had been Susan Pankratz's doing. His railway crew had been replacing a section of track just out of town. She'd walked by one day in early summer and he'd whistled. She wasn't at all like the timid, over-dressed, teenaged grandmothers that Mennonites usually produced. Her hay-coloured hair was curled into long ringlets which she didn't cover with the typical dark kerchief, and she lifted her dress nice and high and dainty when she stepped over the tracks. After that first time, she'd begun dropping by almost every day during his lunch breaks.

There were always other men around at work but he'd had his times alone with Susan, too. Once he'd suggested, only half teasing, that she meet him after her parents thought she was asleep, and to his surprise she had. The quiet walk to Buffalo Bush that night, serenaded by a ditch-full of frogs, the jiggle of the bottom of her breast against his hand on her ribs, her brushing his fingers away from her blouse buttons, timid like a sparrow taking crumbs from a picnic table, and the little pile that her skirt and blouse made on the grass beside the creek in the moonlight, white as cream, came back to him every morning when he woke up. Once the white-coated orderlies had left the room, while the other men grumbled and fought getting up for breakfast, he'd review that lovely banquet from beginning to end and let the familiar feeling swell between his legs. If she knew he wanted a job in

Altwelt she'd persuade her father to get it for him.

The Pankratzes trusted him. Let down their hair for him. One Sunday afternoon, while the women (including Susan— she was only fifteen) washed dishes, Pankratz went so far as to let him in on the workings of the Mennonite West Reserve Waisenamt Fund which he managed. It was a primitive banking system originally set up by Chortitzer Mennonites in Russia to secure the inheritance deposits of widows and orphans. Two hundred thousand dollars was nothing to laugh at, Pankratz had said. Too much money to leave unused. Good collateral for business deals, if you get my drift. You don't have to tell church members everything, he'd added, sipping at the bright sherry. He'd lit a cigarette, drawn the smoke in deep and winked at Charles. God, Pankratz was fortunate, Charles had thought. He'd consider himself lucky if he owned a small house someday before he retired.

GOING HOME

They'd given him a job, but not the one in town. He'd have to teach in the old one-room school in the village a mile to the south. This he'd not expected. What good would that do? Susan wouldn't be there. She attended the town school. Ah—beautiful, silly Susan. There had been a position open in the new town school but the board had recommended some-one else. That insult had stung like the orderly's stick. How could he face the town teachers? To them, being a village teacher was only one step up from a farmer. Besides, you could bet they'd know where he'd spent the last ten months.

And when he got down to teaching it was all mainly problems. The teacherage was meagrely insulated and had more mice in it than a neglected granary, he had to handle thirty-five kids grades one to eight by himself, he didn't know anyone in the village, not that he really cared, and he had to face the thought that he might be stuck doing this for the rest of his life.

But there were also moments that made him forget the yelling and spankings and boredom of hammering information into the unteachable. Eva sweetened it. She was a mature grade eight student who'd begun helping with blackboards and marking and sweeping after four. She was shy, but when she'd come up to his desk with a question she'd just touch her little breasts against his arm while he explained. He'd draw out his explanations as long as he could. Once, in early May when all the kids had finally disappeared, he'd walked her home down the village road. He knew it was daring but he could always explain that he'd been heading out for a stroll in the country anyway.

The air felt innocent, coltish. Flies hummed around the sun's heat in their hair. Some snow still lingered, dirty and insulated with leaves and dead grass, under the clumps of spruce a few of the farmers had planted along the front edges of their properties. They waded through pools of cool air as they walked by the hidden snow.

"Mr. Harder," Eva said, "don't you sometimes wish that you could . . ." A yellow-shafted flicker hammered at a dead poplar branch nearby and Eva looked up at it.

There are a few things I wish I could do with you right now, Charles thought.

"Could what?" he said, suddenly aware of his heartbeat, like the pecking of the flicker. She was pretty. He wanted to look square at her and not take his eyes away. But people in the houses that lined the single road in the village were watching. Be nice to take a shot at them.

"Don't you wish we could be like the birds? You know, flying around free. High up there. Seeing the world way below you. The village, and roads, and people, and horses would be just little specks. Seeing the women in the gardens hoeing but you didn't have to live down there yourself?" She peeked at him. Her eyes were patches of bright sky. Her mouth could make his knees weak and make him forget to breathe. Thy lips are like a thread of scarlet, he thought. Her fat brown pigtail bobbed like the tail of a young horse cantering. She walked almost on tiptoe like that girl in the ballet they'd let some of the better-behaved out to see as a Christmas treat. Light shone through her thin dress when they passed areas of sunlight. It swayed as she stepped, pressed against her thighs at one moment and billowed away the next.

"Eva, would you . . ." he began. A cow mooed in a pasture behind the farmyards. The sun glared through a space between two trees. Its white brilliance hurt his eyes.

"Would I what?" she said with a little smile.

Would you meet me by the creek after dark so I can feed on your lilies? But she probably thinks I am old, grey, ugly. Might laugh at me inside. Might even tell her parents. Actually, that might not be so bad. Chairman of the school board's daughter knocked up. That would make the old tyrant's day, eh? That would be a star in his mighty crown.

"Would you help me put up the crayon pictures tomorrow that we made?" he said. They had reached her house. She nodded and then turned and ran along the edge of the driveway. He stood watching as long as he dared. Her bare arms, bent at the elbow, pumped and flashed, and her bare feet appeared and disappeared like bright strokes of a scythe in the grass.

An Unruly Class

He hated this place. Hated the village people who didn't respect him enough to invite him to supper. Not once in eight months. Often after work as he walked to the teacherage he smelled farmer sausage frying and coffee brewing. He knew people were sitting down to meals it made him ache to think of. Ham, chicken, mashed potatoes soaked in cream and onion gravy, peas and sweet corn canned last fall, preserved crab-apples and blueberry or rhubarb pie. His own meals were pathetic—pancakes without butter because where did a teacher get butter if a neighbour didn't give it to him? Week-old *schnetje* and plum jam. He had plum jam not because of the decency and charity of his neighbours but because he'd bought a case of it at the Altwelt Bergthaler Sewing Circle Bazaar and Bake Sale in October. Proceeds to go to some missionary couple and their five kids in Zaire. Sometimes he'd decide not to eat at all. The thought of forcing down what he'd have to rustle up from the scraps he had lying around his kitchen sickened him.

Most of all he hated their boys. The old overalls, the manure-covered leather boots and stupid, gross, Slavic faces. They couldn't be taught a thing. Didn't give a cow's shitty tail for Goethe or Wordsworth or Newton. And he was snared in this damned occupation. Even asleep he pictured his ugly classroom in riot. Every seat empty. Aisles, schoolyard, streets crowded with howling, writhing bodies.

The real thing was almost as bad as the dream. Class, settle down, he'd say. Nobody listening. Doing everything but. I want you all to . . . What do you want, Jakie? Don't come up here now! I'll come to your desk once I've got things settled down. Okay, everyone, sit down, I have something . . . Aganetha, how many times do I have to tell you to stay in your seat? Don't you ever listen? Hey? Class, we . . . we can't get anything done if . . . Abe Ginter! SIT DOWN! Look, I've . . . Yes, Annie, you can go to the bathroom, but come right . . . Listen here, everyone, I want you all to get busy with your work. Grade eights, work on your "Someone" questions . . . JAKIE!

A PATHETIC JOKE

The boys with the manure on their boots hated him as much as he hated them. Hated how he favoured the girls, especially Eva. How he'd come up behind her and lay his white hands on her shoulders and bend down till his cheek touched her hair. Pretending to study her scribbler while really looking down the front of her blouse. They hated his quiet moods that flared into anger. Jakie still had welts from the spanking he'd gotten. He'd left his seat once too often, teacher had said. He'd had to take off his shirt and stretch out over teacher's desk with his arms hanging down over the end. He'd thought the willow stick would never stop, as if teacher hadn't been able to stop himself once he'd got started. The bruises were thickest around the kidneys and they ran all the way up his back to his shoulder-blades. Some of the boys were almost as big as he was and probably a lot stronger and he made them feel like grade one'ers. One of these days they'd get him.

On Hallowe'en night they did. Three of them. The Klassen boys, Benny, John, and Hank, the oldest kid in school, huddled behind Charles's outhouse. It was dark and cold, and the wind sucked the ugly smell from the full hole and blew it up around them thick and persistent as smoke from a wet poplar fire.

"You go inside," Hank said to John, "and stick the wire through this knothole. Me and Benny'll stay back here. I'll get the wire when it pokes through and Benny'll look out in case he comes." The wind gusted and the stink wafted up to them with new strength through a gap where the outhouse floor didn't cover the hole.

"*Foij*," John whispered. "I'm not sticking my hand in there. I'd rather lick clean a Holstein's tail!"

But he went in anyway. You didn't cross Hank. John remembered the home-made dart in his bare back last summer over an argument about whose turn it was to milk. Hank instructed him again before he went in. "Make the thumbtacks not too tight. Just enough so that the wire won't come loose by itself. And you don't have to have it under the whole opening, you know what I mean? Just where his dink'll hang. And don't worry, he won't be able to see the wire in the dark." They knew Hank was smiling though they couldn't see that in the dark, either.

When John came out they waited. "He'll come around ten," Hank whispered. "Sure as Sunday school. When he sits down, once you hear him pissing, one good yank and *hots dieval* we got him. Like a jack rabbit. He'll try to get loose so we got to pull it good and tight the first time or else he'll get us and it's the reform school." The wind flapped a loose shingle on the outhouse roof and they jumped, ready to run.

When their hearts calmed, Hank said, "We'll give him a couple of good pulls that he'll feel, right Benny? They'll hear him all the way to town! Then we'll give the wire a few turns around this nail and hit the road. And I mean run. Like Siemens's Art in front of the bull. Now, be quiet!" Hank fished in his shirt pocket and pulled out a cigarette and then put it back again.

"But how will he ever get loose?" John asked, peeking around a corner of the outhouse. The teacherage was dark except for a square of yellow lamplight in the kitchen.

"Who cares," Hank said, forgetting to be quiet. "We're going to pull it so tight they'll have to cut off his balls!"

A Terrible Mistake

To top it off, the trustees had been pestering him. Why did he spend so much time on poetry and art instead of more practical stuff, arithmetic and spelling? And shouldn't he be studying the Bible more? Studying the Bible more! Who the hell were they to talk? Like last Sunday night. Poor Mrs. Ginter giving her testimony. Asking the congregation and God to forgive her for being envious of the richer ones in town. Thanking everyone for the second-hand clothes she'd gotten from the good people of the church in the Christmas care basket! Listing her sins for the whole self-righteous herd to sniff at. You think the Friesens or the Wiebes would stand up there and do what they expected her to do? Not in a thousand Sunday nights. The rich didn't have to. They didn't sin.

And making suggestions to him at board meetings that he was too hard on the boys and too friendly with the girls. Them and their pampered kids! One of these days he'd give them something to complain about. Show them what the world was really like. Like he'd had to go through in Minneapolis. He could still feel the jolt of the broom handle in his ribs. The orderly had always carried around a section of it. If he thought you weren't doing a good enough job of the floor or if you hid yourself in a corner, whack, he'd get you.

The white jackets loved to see the pain on your face. He'd gotten so he didn't show any. Just stared at them with steady eyes. That spoiled it for them, sort of. He wasn't always stoic. Not the time some of the patients had made him kneel between the beds. A big one had climbed him like he was a cow. The others had held him. One of them had kept a tight hold of his balls and squeezed if he'd struggled or tried to call out. He'd been sure that the orderlies had known but they hadn't interfered. They must have taken their own kind of pleasure from it.

Tuesday there were three or four of the board members coming to observe him. Maybe he'd pull the gun out of his drawer once they were inside. Give them a scare! Look at this. Look at this. Yeah, you, Penner. That's right. I'm talking to you. How would you like me to . . . That'd give them a scare. Be nice to see them grovel and beg.

THE END OF THE LINE

And now it was all over. He'd never make it to town. He'd been careful not to hit Eva. But Annie was dead. Two of the trustees had fallen too. There was nothing in town for him even if he made it. Charles slowed to a walk. Didn't look over his shoulder. His breath came in quick, hard gasps and each intake knifed his chest. Annie was dead. He knew that. He'd seen the side of her head cave off. She'd been sitting in the front row just at his desk when he'd stepped up to her. A flicker tapped at a fence post further on ahead. Charles took the gun out of his jacket pocket and sat down on one of the rails. He looked out at the pasture. In Minneapolis they never left you alone either, he thought.

A cloud cooled him as it passed and raced on ahead along the tracks toward town. Half a mile away the elevator lost its colour in the cloud's shadow and turned from orange to the yellow of dusty fall grass. The sun lit up and darkened the freshly painted new houses in town as it shifted about behind the broken barrier of clouds. The sorrel mare, standing obedient at its railing, dipped its head down as far as the tether allowed. It couldn't quite reach the short grass that sprouted beside the wooden edge of the sidewalk. Enns and Neustaedter turned to the screen door and stepped back inside. They ordered more coffee and two pieces of cherry pie from Tina while she wiped their table.

CREAM AND WHEY

I'll never make *touareg* now, Walter Regier said to himself. Should have done it when I had the chance. He shook his head and blew at the hair that fell into his eyes, hair almost as thick and black at sixty-one as it had been at twenty. I'd like a glass of that well water, he thought. A glass of that clear, iron-tasting water that dribbles year-round from the galvanized pipe beside the barn. He pictured the moss, green as ripened cheese rind, which grew in the eroded hollow around the well and on the oak footboard his father had put down when the well was sunk. For an acre or more around there the ground was wet clay, soggy. The deep cow tracks were always half full, slurk, schllurk, even in dry times when the pasture grass was shrivelled like Penticton's and you had to be careful not to set the poplar brush on fire. It felt so cool on your bare feet there you might have been wading in an April creek.

His mouth and his insides itched with dryness as if he were Parmesan or a barrel of the Janitor In A Drum that Frieda used on the cement floor in the late afternoon when the raking troughs had been cleaned and the wedges and rounds set on the shelves in the ripening room. I'd have no trouble falling asleep on a cot in there, he thought, where it's damp and smells like must and mould and whey. When he'd come back from up north because his father had left him part of the farm, he'd married Frieda, sold the farmland, and with the money built a cheese factory. In the first few years after starting the business he'd hated its pungencies, but they'd grown on him over time. It got to the point where, on Sundays, when he was still attending, the unclean smells in the church—the toilet downstairs, the varnished benches in the summer heat, the mothball stink of the old people's suits and dresses—made him long for that room with its rows of aging wheels of cheese.

I used to like cutting the winter wood with Dad, Walter thought. That was always a good time when I was younger. Walter was the oldest and it had been up to him to help choose which poplars to cut and to snag the dragging chains around the felled trees while his father handled the horses. And later, once they'd bucked out the logs and loaded them and carted them to the yard and thrown them down in a lopsided pile like pick-up-sticks, he was in charge of feeding the buzz-saw that stood by the barn year-round. On those days he and his father got along because his father didn't have time to preach and Walter got a share in authority. His younger brothers and sisters had to listen to his orders about stacking the billets that spilled out from under the rusted saw blade.

So, yes, there had been some good times at home. When the first frosts came, for instance. They'd pile split poplar from floor to ceiling beside and under the stairs in the dirt basement, and three or four times a day they'd toss chunks of the Old Chum-smelling wood into the furnace. The big steel door, two feet square with a creature embossed on it, half scaly dragon and half naked woman, creaked when you opened it. The cavity behind the door was so big that a twelve-year-old could have made his bed in there and lain down full-length. In cold weather the embers glowed red and white, waiting to be fed. When he felt the heat and saw the roar of the flames, Walter found it hard to believe the story of Daniel in King Darius's fire.

Wonder what I'll say to Dad when I see him again, he thought. That's if I'm going there. I almost wish I didn't have to meet him. I can't believe he'll be any wiser. When he was older, starting about the age of sixteen, Walter had begun to hate his father. It might have started even earlier but till then it had been less evident. Walter hadn't called it hate. Told himself he loved his parents very much, just didn't get along with them. Couldn't tell them what he really felt inside, bunged up with something as sticky and gummy as clay in the horses' hooves. Couldn't be himself. His father was forever preaching, obsessed with right and wrong, black and white, what he called hell and heaven. Once, on the way home from Sunday night church service, he'd pulled the horses up to Miller's Pool Hall and tried handing out tracts to everyone inside. He'd stop men on the street who were smoking and lecture them about tobacco and alcohol. Ask them, do you think people will smoke in heaven? And then Walter couldn't stand it anymore. Had to get away.

One of his friends worked in the CNR freight yard and had landed him a job with the company. Building the line to Churchill. That had been an eye-opener. How narrow the Steinbach people had seemed to him then, narrower than the light that shone under his door when he was alone and protected and warm at night. He'd realized that Swedes and Norwegians and Frenchmen and native Indians and Chinese had other thoughts about food and drink and church and women. About fathers and sons. About how a man could and couldn't behave. You didn't ask people if they were Christians. You didn't challenge a man about whether he had nightly devotions or whether he worked on Sundays. To drink a dozen beer wasn't sin, just ask Jean Einarson who, when he drank, danced with the loose women, it was just an activity like other activities. Like milking cows or getting your hair cut. With drinking you felt sick in the morning when you went to work and so maybe you wouldn't do it for a week or two, but it wasn't sin. Playing blackjack payday in the railcar at The Pas siding with Sharky Mireau was a sure way to cut down on your savings but it wasn't sin. And spending the night in a railcar with one of the native women who hung around the camps evenings maybe was foolish, maybe even dangerous because she might have a native boyfriend who'd come looking for you, but it wasn't sin. Like the time Raymond Flett pulled a knife on him in front of the Swan River Community Hall. He and Marina Flett had been off the dance floor too long and Raymond had seen them coming out of the bush. He'd got off lucky that time and talked his way out of it with words and a case of beer. But nobody would have called it sin.

Sin wasn't cut and dried the way his father's life had been. And churches were there to let you confess and forget, not to watch every little action and pounce on you if you strayed. In The Pas, many fathers, even those who were regular church-goers, drank with their older sons. Got silly together. Told jokes about the farmer's daughter and the salesman, or Father McNally and something being tighter than a nun's box, both the kid and the old man, without guilt. Steinbachers, Mennonites, had it all screwed up.

If I end up in the hospital I wonder if Rebecca will come to see me, Walter thought. If she doesn't it'll be because she's afraid to bump into Frieda. Maybe I'll never get to see her again.

Would Frieda and Rebecca be all right once he was gone? They'd miss him at first, at least Rebecca would, but after a while maybe they'd be grateful. They'd finally be allowed to forget, though in the last years it hadn't been as bad. People had stopped interfering. Grown tired of worrying about their salvation. Monday to Friday Walter lived with Frieda in the two-and-a-half-storey farmhouse two miles east of Steinbach on the road toward St. Anne. Weekends he drove the refrigerator truck into Winnipeg to Stanislov's Dairy on Higgins and for the next two days he stayed with Rebecca in her basement suite on Henry. There'd been problems with this arrangement, especially the first two years, but by now things had mellowed and the *ménage à trois* had gone along as well as could be expected, considering that two of them lived in Steinbach. Righteous people stop forgiving even before seven times, why should this be any different? So the objections of their relatives and acquaintances and neigh-bours had drained away like old milk down the drainage ditch. Anything else took too much energy. Now people simply left them alone. Didn't visit them anymore or invite them to supper or to family gatherings.

It had taken Walter and Frieda a few years to realize they couldn't have kids. That had been hard, especially for Frieda. She'd changed with that knowledge. Become more morose and less aware of him. At least on the surface. She might have loved him still, but it didn't show. When they'd first been married, Frieda had taken pride in setting up a meal like the restaurants did with a variety of courses. They didn't eat at restaurants often, but when they went to a good one, Frieda took note of it all. She was a curd press, squeezing everything she could out of it. She loved the showiness. The clean chequered table-cloths, the candle-light, the formal waiters, the strange sauces and breads and rice, noodle and meat dishes, and the foreign wines and beers. Drinking in

Steinbach, if you were at all respectable, was *verboten* but he'd never worried much about that from the time he'd left home. Not till he'd started his own business. Then, later, a few years after their troubles began, he'd become less anxious about respectability again and begun drinking when he felt like it.

His father had once been accused in a brotherhood meeting of drinking beer and that had almost ended in his excommunication. He'd been on his annual fishing trip in the Whiteshell and a few church members happened to see him sipping what they thought was beer though it was really brown-bottled ginger-beer. Since the lake was isolated the accusation carried more weight. Such a perfect place to hide a sin, they must have reasoned. Like truckers who never had affairs closer than five hundred miles from home.

So, when it became clear that they couldn't have children, Frieda lost interest in life, in their marriage. Her meals deteriorated. There were no salads to start the supper anymore and no soup entrées or fancy dishes. Just ham and potatoes and corn or peas or beef roast and potatoes and corn or peas like the rest of the farmers' wives' suppers.

And their sex life headed downhill with their meals. Frieda found excuses in bed when he'd turn to her. Didn't make sleepy humming sounds when he put his hand on her breast or nuzzle back toward him when he pressed his erection against her. That had been worse than anything. There'd been a time when it was good. She humoured him, even enjoyed it. Sometimes, though not often, three times a night. In the evening it would be mutual. Lively. They'd both romp around and make a game of it. She'd say no but her eyes would say yes and they'd fight naked with pillows or she'd strip-tease for him. At night, when he came back from the washroom or just woke up feeling horny, she'd let him do what he wanted as long as it didn't get complicated and she didn't have to be active. Sometimes they'd even make love in the morning before breakfast though he'd have to start the cheese curdling by seven. In those days he missed her when he left the house. Fridays on his trips into Winnipeg he could hardly wait to get back to Steinbach.

That's where Rebecca came in, Walter thought, because later I must have been very unhappy. I should have left her alone, let her know I wasn't going to give in to those feelings. But God I loved her. So incredibly beautiful. Thin but sort of comfortable and soft. Skin soft and creamy smooth as butter. And so white. I couldn't touch her enough. My breath just stuck in my throat when I'd think about her. I know, I know. I had a business to build and a marriage to work on and fix somehow, but Jesus, I couldn't stop myself from wanting her.

Rebecca was Frieda's younger sister. There'd been something between them even during the time he was courting Frieda. She'd aroused him in a way Frieda couldn't. Maybe it was that Rebecca loved him and he couldn't resist being needed. He didn't know. Maybe it was their personalities. Frieda was whey, Rebecca cream. Frieda content to spend her mornings preening the house and yard and lounging away the afternoons reading, but Rebecca restless. Rebecca would turn the radio on and then off again, on and off like that every few minutes, or pace between the kitchen table and the window when she came to visit, while she still visited them, before she got the job as secretary at the Winnipeg Grain Exchange. Frieda keeping the kitchen and garden just so, picking the crabgrass out of the flower-bed beneath the front window and sweeping cobwebs from under the eaves with a straw broom, Rebecca itching to take one of the horses riding.

He'd sensed that Rebecca had stayed single because of him. Couldn't separate the obligation of starting a family from the irrational hope that someday he'd be available. She'd only been fifteen when he'd first met Frieda, but she'd had the guile and shape of a twenty-year-old. Breasts as full as her sister's, eyes clear and grey as the water from the artesian in the pasture, and arms smooth like poplar branches and as long and slender.

The stars were out as bright as Walter had ever seen them. The Big Dipper, empty as the curdling tank at the end of the day, each of its stars white cream cheese, seemed to be pouring its emptiness over him. She was hot for me that first day I called on Frieda, Walter thought. She flirted with me at the door when I came. She said, "You're here for Frieda? Why not me?" Her eyes had looked square into his, laughing and reprimanding at the same time, speaking something they both understood later. Just as you knew more about horseback riding and the broadness and slipperiness of the horse's back when you'd fallen a few times. They'd known that she was too young. That he was her sister's. Yet, whenever they met, even after he was married, she pursued him and he didn't object. She'd appear when he happened to be alone for a few minutes and he'd find reasons to touch her long, brown hair or brush her shoulder with his fingers or chest. A few times he'd pulled her onto his lap and, when she didn't object, pressed his knee up between her thighs. She'd just giggled and pressed back before jumping up. She'd wanted a share of him, not consciously, probably not in any way that she could have spelled out, but the way a calf wants an udder, he thought.

If I hadn't had coffee with her that first time at Eaton's maybe it never would have happened, Walter thought. Most of the time Rebecca hadn't preoccupied him, though on his weekend trips he'd had his fantasies. But that was no different from any man, surely. Be nice to take her for ice cream at the pavilion in Assiniboine Park and then go see the zoo. Maybe tour the Legislative Building together. Shoulder to shoulder through those wide, cool halls with their great oak doors. And stand, just as you walked into the building, under that buffalo, with her leaning back against him, all that bulk hanging over them. Get stormed in at Winnipeg and have to spend the night in her suite. Her in her nightgown as she makes up the couch. Coffee together around her breakfast table and sleep and night still thick around her. Be nice. But, of course he couldn't be seen that way, not with his wife's sister.

He'd been raking leaves on an October afternoon at the farmhouse when it had hit him. I love Rebecca. Loved her when I was calling on Frieda. Just before he'd realized this he'd been thinking about his wife. He was lonely. Why did she always find separate work from him? If he raked leaves outside, she washed floors inside. Never failed. If he was refinishing kitchen cabinets upstairs, she did laundry downstairs. They were never together now except at night, and then they were tired as a rule and went straight to bed, the words they didn't speak keeping them awake for a while, loud and silly as a retarded adult's. I loved Rebecca then already, he'd thought again. I loved Rebecca and liked Frieda. I couldn't have Rebecca because she was too young, but I loved her in secret and hid it even from myself. I shouldn't have married Frieda. It was Rebecca.

The idea that he had loved Rebecca from the beginning had disturbed his sense of belonging and he had thought of how wind scatters a loose pile of leaves. In the first moments when this was occurring to him he thought it was another one of his fantasies but no, not this one, this one got hold of him in a different way. It flooded him, unavoidable as the time when three days' worth of milk had swooshed over the processing floor. His helper had knocked one of the legs from under the holding vat, and there it was, all over the place.

Not long afterwards he'd dropped in on her where she worked and they'd spent the afternoon coffee break together. After she'd finished at five o'clock, just as he'd imagined, they'd walked through the Legislative Building. Both of them had marvelled at the fossils in the two-foot-thick slabs of limestone that made up the building's walls and they had joked about the fossils inside.

Over time he'd found excuses to stay in the city the odd night. His business was doing well enough for him to spend a bit of money when he felt like it, he told Frieda, and he didn't have to be in the plant every Saturday. Frieda wasn't interested in joining him and though she wondered why he was staying over, he simply explained that he had to get away from Steinbach once in a while. That he'd made a friend in Winnipeg who was a supervisor at Stanislov's and they really got along well. This guy actually pestered him to stay more often. They shot pool together, he said, and went to the Occidental for a few beer on Saturday afternoon. He had earned the right to have some fun now and then, hadn't he, and she hadn't been able to say anything.

Rebecca had been strangely willing. That had surprised him, but not for long. He'd realized that he'd been right about her longing for him. Just today, she'd say when he worried about being discovered. Just stay tonight and then maybe we'll have to stop seeing each other or maybe you can stop staying nights. We'll see. But don't let's talk about it right now, okay?

And though he'd known that they'd be discovered sometime, that the world, even their closet of it, hummed and clicked to laws of probability, he had let his fears ride. Till the day Frieda had found his poems. They were little verses that he took very seriously, that he wrote from somewhere he had found, surprised, in himself, as eagerly as his father had read the Bible. Mainly they had to do with Rebecca's body. Her low laughter like water, the way she stood, with the toe of her right foot just touching the ground, weight on the left foot, the creamy whiteness of her thighs, the black curls between her legs.

The poems Frieda found were copies. Rebecca had the originals. He'd expected that Frieda was safely in the house making supper and had left them on his office desk while he went to fill an emergency order. There was a wedding at the Steinbach Emmanuel Free Church and they needed cheese. The success of his business depended on his readiness to take such orders on short notice. When he'd come back, she was bent over his desk and she hadn't looked up at him. He'd sensed the tension, slow, heavy as cream. As she walked by him in the doorway she'd whispered, how could you, and he'd felt the slice of each syllable.

But they hadn't split up, except in ways that were less visible to the public. Christians didn't get divorced. It was bad for business. They'd bought single beds and slept in separate rooms. They'd eaten their meals together but in silence. At first he'd wanted to explain, felt the burden of defending his actions to her, and she'd seemed interested in knowing what had happened. But whenever they moved to such topics as their meals and sex life and Frieda's remoteness, she balked and criticized him. He'd been dishonest and distant, too, she'd said. It was largely his fault and if he couldn't admit that, she didn't want to discuss it.

In the rush of the moment Walter had decided he'd stop seeing Rebecca altogether. He had to forget her now and concentrate on fixing things up at home. But the need to inform her about Frieda and him was there. He'd promised Frieda he wouldn't see her sister but already on his next delivery into the city, in a moment so sudden it surprised him to find himself driving in the direction of her house, he'd determined that he had to tell her everything. Had to. They'd held each other and promised to remain friends despite what people might say and despite his commitment to his wife and the business. We have to see each other, they'd said. We can't quit just like that, not now. We love each other. You have to at least come here and let me know what she's thinking, Rebecca had argued. You can come for an hour at lunch or right after your deliveries on Fridays and Frieda doesn't have to know. Frieda staying aloof and bitter, eventually he'd slipped into the habit of spending every weekend with Rebecca.

I feel so dry, Walter thought, so dry I could crack and blow away. The air smelled like cut clover and cheese. He focussed on the Big Dipper again to see if it had shifted since the last time he'd looked. Maybe it's because I've lost a lot of blood, he thought. I'm sure I have. It's wet around my hips and that'll be blood. It wouldn't be any good like this even if they could save me. It's probably better if they don't. The truck's loaded right up. When they lift it maybe my legs will come off. They'll never save the legs. Should have been more careful but I couldn't really see in the dark when I jacked it up. It must have been leaning more than I thought.

Because of the truck's tilt, many of the cream cans had tipped. Some of the cans had no cream left in them and it was still leaking from others. The cream found places to run out of the truck box. Wheels of cheese had fallen off their shelves and there was a sharp smell of wet, old cheddar in the air. There'd been plenty of rain that spring and the water table was high. Run-off gurgled in the ditch a few feet from Walter's head. In the dark, a red and white trickle pushed down the slope, diluted by the ditch-water flowing toward the city.

A PICTURE OF JESUS

At such times Principal Wiebe felt like quitting his job, felt like moving out of Altwelt to Winnipeg or maybe Brandon where everybody's dog yap yap yap didn't know him and bother itself every minute with what he was up to. There'd been a minor problem in the boys' room over the lunch break—a broken door, a plugged toilet, a cracked seat. He'd been forced to ask the janitor to clean up the yellow pools that had gathered in the low spots on the floor and the janitor had looked at him like he'd just as soon walk out of the school for good. Clots of toilet paper had been floating in one of the stalls and some suspicious darker clumps that he didn't want to think about.

Kids who'd been seen nearby couldn't remember anything, the staff thought it was up to him and wouldn't lift a finger and, worst of all, he'd had to go through the sort of public investigation with intercoms, memos and locker searches that made him suspicious for weeks that everyone in the place was laughing at him. But Wiebe had done his duty, announced over the P.A. that anyone with information should report to his office. He hadn't been hopeful. Just a preliminary waste of time. But when Thomas showed up at the office door, it looked like things might click for once.

Neither of them spoke for a while. Thomas saw the thin, black hand in the round clock above the picture of Jesus tick off the seconds. It jerked and strained forever forward. Forced air from the furnace starting up fluttered the beige embroidered cloth on the coffee table with the lamp on it. Wiebe shook his head and pressed the palm of his hand back against the grain of his crew cut. He looked at Thomas who stood with arms stretched down in front of him and his hands folded. Thomas's black eyes were bright chips of coal that a conscientious son would sweep up after filling the booker.

"I want to get this straight," Wiebe said. "You were there when it happened?" He lifted a sheet of foolscap onto the neat stack of papers at the edge of the table to his left and set his elbows down.

"Yes," Thomas answered, not leaning either forward or backward, "I was." He reached his hand behind his head and ran a finger down the parting in his ducktail. Not a hair out of place. Pale October sunlight filtered through a bald spot in the grey cap of cloud and the shadows of branches from the ash tree outside the window played on the attendance record and on the black pebbled cover of the Bible that Wiebe used for morning ceremonies. He'd used that Bible every morning since he'd started this job twenty-two years ago. It had its own exact spot on the desk. No other book or file ever rested on it. Wiebe made certain of that.

"And you know their names?" He stared unblinking at Thomas but Thomas didn't shuffle or look away.

"I think I know them all," he said. A drop of Brylcreem trickled down his neck. He reached up to wipe it off. The wet smear felt cool. "At least I saw two of them, the ones that looked over the top of the stall where I was sitting. But I recognized the other one, too. By his voice." Wiebe waited. Thomas uncrossed his hands and stood silent. His hands and arms hung down loose and lifeless as cows' tails when there were no flies. His eyes, suddenly tiring, reminded Wiebe of dugout water when a cloud covers the sun. In a moment all the cow tracks, underwater insects and submerged shore grass vanish.

"And you're not going to tell me their names?" Wiebe said. He tilted to one side to let the sun fall on Thomas's face.

"No. I would like to but I can't." Thomas pried at something in his teeth and then looked at his fingernail before wiping it under the pocket of his orange shirt. "I don't want you to punish them," he said. The sun burned his eyes. He blinked and squeezed them shut.

Wiebe cleared his throat. He started to speak but his voice squeaked and he had to start again. "So what do you think I should do? Just let them off? Let them wreck the school around our ears? Eh?" he said, taking a quick look at the clock on the wall. He watched two seconds tick off on the second hand before he shifted his eyes back to the boy.

The branches on the desk waved as if something outside were shaking the tree. Raspberry, strawberry, jelly and jam. Waves of grit from the skipping rope pelted the window. A bell rang. Silhouettes scurried past the smoky office door window with PRINCIPAL written on it in a straight line of black, fat, four-inch letters.

"I would like you to strap me instead," Thomas said. He had to raise his voice over the noise from the hall. He leaned his head in the same direction Wiebe had moved to get his eyes out of the sun. Wiebe toyed with a corner of the Bible cover, thinking.

Feet trampled around in the hall and locker doors

slapped shut. The hubbub swelled, receded and died out. The drone of teachers' voices from the classrooms close to the office mixed in the hall with the thuck, thack of Wiebe's belt. The janitor had cut the strap for Wiebe out of a combine belt he'd fished from under the wire fence at Klassen's Auto Wrecking on the way to work one morning. There was lots of the stuff scattered around among the rusted cars. After a while, Thomas stepped out of the office, closed the door, and hurried toward his room with his hands in the back pockets of his corduroys.

In the late afternoon, Thomas's mother, Susan, stood at the counter by the kitchen window, cutting dough into bun-sized pieces and listening to the "Back to the Bible" broadcast. She never listened to any other station but CFAM. She loved the afternoon religious programs and the daily funeral announcements. She liked the way the announcer who read out the information about the people who had died made his voice low and respectful. As if he were personally hurt. She knew most of the people who had died the day before and there was a flush of pleasure at being alive to hear the familiar names. The radio sat on the fridge and odds and ends collected around it: pins, pennies, rubber jar rings. It was a cheap AM model she'd ordered through the Eaton's catalogue a dozen years ago and because there was no tone control the man's voice coming from it sounded too strained and treble. Often Susan had had to adjust the dial to find the place with the least annoying static. But she'd grown accustomed to it and it didn't bother her anymore.

The acrid yeast smell from the baking in the oven comforted her as if the room had been filled with singing angels and harp music. She loved Pastor Barber, too. His messages were so meaningful and helpful. But as much as she'd like to, she couldn't just stand there and listen and so she never heard all of what he said. There were always interruptions. A woman raising six kids was a busy woman, she thought, and she couldn't always be listening, not even if it was the Lord.

Mr. Regier usually came home late. Between 9:00 and 10:00. After he'd done his bookkeeping and they were in bed she'd tell him about the sermon. Henry, you should have heard Pastor Barber's talk today! It was wonderful! Just wonderful! He spoke on the twenty-third psalm! Won't it be wonderful when we're in heaven, Henry? Then all our sorrows will be over! Sometimes I can hardly wait.

They often talked then about the streets of gold and each person in heaven having his own planet and whether all their children would be there with them. Oh, let's hope that they'll all follow Jesus, Susan would say and Henry would reassure her. Teach your children in the way they should go and when they are old they will not depart from it.

Today the text was Proverbs 11:29. He that troubleth his own house shall inherit the wind. While she listened to the radio, she pinched and pulled pieces from the main dough with the tips of her fingers and sliced at it with the butcher knife, rolled the lumps under her palms on the counter, and placed them nicely spaced on the big, black, greased pans. The knife swished through the warm, moist, cream-coloured mass and clicked on the arborite countertop. It was a handy knife. Henry used it during pig slaughtering to cut the jugular vein and scrape the hair, she used it to slab the blocks of deer soap she made downstairs every fall, and it had gutted a thousand chickens. To keep it razor-sharp she honed it on the large front element of the kitchen stove.

When she was almost finished cutting the dough she saw Thomas walking up the driveway. He should wear a hat in this weather, she thought. He never wore one. It messed up his ducktail. She heard him hang up his school jacket in the closet in the garage. He stepped into the kitchen as she slashed at the dough with the knife. She turned to smile at him. His face startled her. His mouth was opening slowly. Wider than it should. His eyes were fixed on the knife. Suddenly he brought his fists down on the countertop, looking away from the knife at the ceiling. "Mom, the knife," he whispered. "Put it away, okay, Mom?" He rocked back and forth, his eyes still looking up.

Her eyes filled with not knowing what to do. She still had dough to cut. "Thomas! Why should I hide it?" she said. She pulled at the cutlery drawer but kept the knife at her side.

"I don't know," Thomas said, his voice too high, out of control. "I don't know." And then he was sobbing. "I dunno, I'm scared." He laid his head on his bare arms on the counter, and his head and shoulders shook with crying as if they'd never stop. Susan looked at his neat, combed, thick head of hair and the wisps of finer black hair on his arms. She waited, the drawer half opened. What was it, what was in her son she waited for? And then she saw.

"I'm afraid what I might do." His words were quiet as birds when they fall asleep but his mouth was near the arborite of the countertop and they echoed in her head and blew there like the wind, stranger and darker than any wind she had imagined in heaven. "I love you and I don't know why I feel that but I do. Will you just put it away, please. Put it away, Mom." Thomas jerked open the kitchen door and ran back out of it, ran downstairs to his room.

Susan heard his bedroom door slam. She slipped the knife into the drawer. The larger lump of uncut dough lay on the counter, puffed up till the yeast in it was spent, and then it fell flat as a pancake.

Thomas filled the old pail with chunks of black coal from the coal room and lugged it over to the booker furnace. This was his job after four. On the second try he got the pail up beside the little round door where the coal went in. The door's steel handle, shiny from rubbing, was too hot to touch. He slapped at it with his free hand to uncock it, waited a second for his fingers to cool and then jerked at it again to open the door. He stood on tiptoe, careful of his orange shirt-front, and peered down into the hole. The smoke was grey-white and it curled and billowed in the stove's fat, empty belly. Underneath, hidden, was the glowing fire. Like the fire in hell, Thomas thought. Orange heat that would blister your hand in a moment and singe off your hair in a twinkling. He breathed deep and blew down to disturb the smoke so he'd be able to see the embers glowing. An oil-thick creosote cloud belched up into his face, through his perfect hair, toward the ceiling, and spread from joist to joist in a sluggish wind.

BAPTISM

One brittle morning after a blizzard some of us Regier kids got up early to shovel the snowbank that blocked the driveway. It was usually my job to stoke the coal booker but today it had already been done and the floor around the five-gallon MCPA pail was warm, an arctic hotspring. Lifting the toilet seat always took all my courage, like sniffing deeply from an ammonia bottle, but once you got used to the smell of a brimming five gallons that should have been carried out five days ago, it was all tolerable, even comfortable. I sat there listening to Peter Olsen's "Farm Broadcast," the sound magnified by the tin exhaust pipe behind the toilet, and I would have liked to stay an hour. But the shovelling had to be done before breakfast so my father could exit at his regular time (time is money) and we kids would be ready when the bobsled arrived.

The bobsled brought the village kids to school in town even after a minor blizzard because our retiring bus driver was unreliable. He would get the regular Greyhound school bus stuck even on days when my father managed to plow his way through the country all day long with only a station wagon. So, because of the sled, blizzards like this were a real treat. On second thought, they weren't entirely, and I realize that history tells us lies. It is tempting to remember only the pleasures of the storm because I intend to emphasize the fun our family had working together early in the morning on a crisp winter day. The arcadian atmosphere lends itself perfectly to the approaching shift in tone, to the dramatic/ironic contrast of the cistern story to follow. But then I remember what happened to Eddy Friesen on the sled the year before.

Eddy was standing on the narrow wooden lip outside the sled's side wall, facing the kids who were on the inside, and he was swinging his body far out the way a sailor balances a skiff. The horses shifted gears or we hit a bump, and Eddy slipped down underneath, between the front and back runners. Four thousand pounds thumped over him. Everybody screamed till the horses finally stopped and then were silent as they looked back at the corpse and the fat white chalk mark across his blue jacket. Mr. Ginter scrambled back toward him as we watched, expecting the snow to redden and guts to bubble out from underneath Eddy's parka. Then suddenly he stood up, dazed, unhurt. The snow was so soft that he'd simply been pushed down underneath it by the sled's weight. Later, when he tiptoed ceremoniously through the classroom door, he whispered loudly enough for everyone to hear that Dr. Driedger said he was okay. It was the middle of Health period and we were studying safety, I think.

Before we started to work, my father pried the cement lid off the cistern with the iron bar that used to keep the barn door closed. He showed us the ice around the hole and warned us to be careful. And then while we worked, carrying the crumbling snow to the cistern block by block, in single file, we asked him about his job. About the impassable country roads in winter, about freezing to death if you got stuck, about vicious dogs, about a hundred other things that excite kids. He humoured us. Exaggerated until we couldn't stop laughing. The way my mind wants to see this picture, the air should swell now as the line of workers sways in step and chants full-bodied Cossack harmonies. Snow White and the Seven Dwarfs in Russia.

We were finished by the time my mother called us in for breakfast, but I stayed behind alone to try out the big aluminum shovel. Father's shovel. Phallic shovel? Or something from the collective unconscious? Actually, I don't think the spade is one of Jung's shaping symbols. Not noble enough.

To get back to the story, I was making the snow edges perfect which the others had left jagged. And I loved the rhythm of the work. I was strong, important, finishing a job by myself with the big shovel. Exhilarated, running with the loads, balancing, juggling the burden of snow and sliding the last few feet to dump-truck-tilt them into the ice-water.

At the tail end of one such run I suddenly knew I was in trouble. My forward momentum was carrying me too far. Nothing I could do to stop. I flung my arms apart but the hole was three feet wide and they had no strength stuck out horizontally like the crossmember of a clothes-line pole. I slipped in, far down underneath the cement floor like a seal at the ice-edge. I don't remember the cold though it must have numbed me. I just felt wetness at my throat and wrists and saw light back in the direction from which I'd come. At that instant I knew I was a dead man, but I didn't even have time to be horrified before a surge of water returning from the far side of the cistern pushed me back and squirted me half-way up out of the hole, as if strong arms had dipped me in and jerked me out. I kicked and flapped my legs, and felt my nails and wrists slip. I was sliding back in! No! I rolled over in desperation. At the same moment I brought up one leg and jammed it against the other side of the hole. And I was safe. Safe!

My first thought was to make sure my mistake wasn't discovered. I searched the ice for signs of the struggle, brushed away some marks with the garage straw broom, rushed down to my bedroom to change. I explained at the breakfast table that I had really had to go to the bathroom, badly.

"We've been waiting for you so we could start devotions," my father said, holding the Bible in one hand and looking at me over his black bifocals like he always did when he was displeased. The rest of the family let me know in their silent ways that I had committed the unpardonable sin, making them wait for their porridge. I apologized but inside I was thinking that I was much wiser. I have joined the ranks of the water rat, I thought. I know now how gophers feel when boys drown them out for their two-cent tails. Later on I realized that I was unusually moved when all hands were lost at sea in the newspaper and that in unfathomable ways I knew more than a little about surfing.

THE ICE PATCH FIELD

White air pockets exploded under our four-buckled greaves
and icicles skittered ahead of us like mice on linoleum.
Richard Stoez and I were ice-breaking our way home over
Stealer Remple's cultivated field on a day made only slightly
more bearable by the fact that Miss Harder let us listen to
the Yankees-Boston final on Billy Pohl's new eight-
transistor Philips radio. It was a gift from the *Tribune*
people for his five new daily customers in September. They
sent a representative out specially from Winnipeg and he
made the presentations at J. Wheelers and Sons Transfer
Co. by the truck where they always unloaded the bundles
of *Free Press* and *Tribune*. But now, after four, we were
Goliaths thundering down the Valley of Elah, let the world
beware. After a while, Richard got back on the gravel road
and slung stones at the green insulators. If you connected

with one it shattered like ice. I stayed in the field, skidding over wet patches about as gracefully as Eddy Shack pumping down left wing.

Baseball and sex have nothing in common, I know that, but they are forever linked in my mind from that particular afternoon in room 7A of the Parkside Elementary School. A bunch of us grade seven boys hovered around the crackle of the announcer's nasal play-by-play and leaned on the counter at the back of the room in a nook that was flanked on one side by the yellow varnished cloakroom doors and on the other by the high windows facing west. The bottom halves were frosted glass so you couldn't see outside, but from up above sunlight streamed down like Mother Holle's gold on Johnnie, the class bully, on Snapper, whose hair dripped grease and who instigated every ruckus without ever getting caught, on Long Tall Sally, Puke, and Feather, and on the girls quietly drawing in pairs at their desks, whose whispers and print dresses clothed the room in comfort like Christmas music Saturday morning under the quilt. Their pretty complacence overwhelms me even now with such longing. Life's promises unfulfilled. The ache of heart and bones for a girl you're not supposed to love. Anima projections, I later learned, but it wasn't, just.

Richard hated sports and stood on the far side of the room by the mural which covered the blackboard along one whole wall. He was Miss Harder's *artiste célèbre* and he patiently brushed new fire and orange chaos into the mushroom cloud that dominated our "Nuclear War," a project the class was preparing to send to the Canadian National Exhibition's Public Schools Art Contest in Toronto. The cloud dilated and billowed in the distance behind an unsuspecting farmer on a John Deere and cultivator in a blackening field, behind cows, heads low, hay in their mouths, and behind the farmer's wife milking a Holstein. Nothing ever nearly so beautiful had ever been created, ever, and we knew it would bring in a first. Later when we saw the third prize ribbon we agreed they must have made a mistake.

I've been filling in this picture of the sun on the kids and the mural at least in small part to put off dealing with what this story's really about. It's simple enough to paint a clear picture of that grade seven class on that afternoon, but how do you shift from the kind of sex that floats thick and unrecognized everywhere like flecks of dust in a hayloft to the kind that shows you, as if for the first time, the dizzy rocking beneath your feet?

At this point in the series I am Mickey Mantle. I've already hit four home runs all told, two more than Maris, and with the teams tied at three games apiece I'll have to slug at least one more to bring the pennant home.

Sometime during the disastrous eighth inning, probably when Hal Smith's homer scored Dick Groat and Roberto Clementes and everyone in the room temporarily lost interest in the game, Johnnie Pankratz started drawing his graffiti over my Rockwell reverie. He scratched in all the private parts: similes for pubic hair, the penis's colours and purposes, the proximity of rectum to vagina.

I recoiled from his vulgarity. He had me cornered. What could I say to the loudest, toughest kid in the school? "Here's five cents. Go buy yourself brain surgery"? He would have dug in my pockets for more change while he continued his scatalogue. Or maybe, "I'm not interested. Go bug Fuzz"? For one thing, his description mesmerized me, and for another, he would have made it hell for me: grabbed my testicles, for instance, and squeezed till I begged for mercy or agreed to call Corny and Gary "Asshole" and "Prick" right on the spot. Those two malcontents stuck to Pankratz like Reverend Brunk to his predictions of fire.

All the years that I knew Johnnie, I didn't stand a chance against him and he managed to get his own way in everything. In kindergarten he persuaded Tammy Krahn, the prettiest girl in class I thought then, to strip off all her clothes and crawl through the room at lunch-time pretending to be a horse. I stood there dumbstruck when she came through the girls' washroom door on all fours. All she was wearing was one of those complicated white garters for her stockings, the kind that fasten at the waist with a belt.

In grade three he brought playing cards and convinced me to convince the teacher to let me sit next to him in a corner by the library books. There he forced me to play rummy with him. I was scared stiff that Miss Barg would see us. And my conscience plagued me because my parents believed it was a sin to play with this particular kind of cards. Old Maid and Fish cards were okay, but those with king and queen pictures were satanic.

All through grade school it was the same thing. Johnnie was my nemesis and I was a sucker. But he's come into his own, now. Early afternoon, he's probably pumping iron in the Milhaven gym. Serving time for embezzlement. Sometime after he flunked grade ten he joined the marines and later briefly managed the Stratford Credit Union in Perth County, Ontario. What he's chasing now probably doesn't wear panties or at least won't admit to it.

"It comes out all sticky and soft," Johnnie said, nudging my shoulder. He was short but heavyset and he blocked any retreat I'd try to make. Magwich, head shaved and round as the globe on teacher's desk, about to turn Pip on his head. I pretended to ignore him and listened hard to the radio.

"Even your mom and dad do it." He knew how to hit home. This was more dangerous than the pea-shooter we made in grade six loaded with a #7 needle and weighted on one end with Scotch tape so it would fly straight. We generally used it only on the bulletin board but once I tried to shoot close to Abram Penner and pierced his ear. It dangled there for a long minute while he screamed around the room before he had the nerve to pull it out.

"Your dad sticks it in the hole between your mom's legs," he smirked.

My mom's hole? I'd never thought of her as having one. I'd seen crude drawings in the washroom so I knew approximately what was down there, but somebody sticking something in it? Impossible. Not my parents. My head reeled. The red and white tiles floated, waned, undersized and distant, and then surged upward to such a size and weight that they dragged the whole school building downward into the clay.

"They don't do that." I sounded a lot like a hungry sheep.

"Sure they do. That's how they make babies. That's how come you're here, stupid." He laughed, silently so Miss Harder wouldn't notice, and the others joined in. A Rabelaisian choir. Of course I hadn't known. How would I? How could they know such things?

I'm not sure which I loathed more at that moment, the brief vision of my mother on her back naked and exposed, or my strange ignorance. They say that kids forget easily, but I don't recall any of the ninth inning of the game, not even when Mazeroski slapped Ralph Terry's slider over the left field wall and won it for the Bucs.

At one point the furrows widened into a sheet of marble, ice, fifty yards long, parallel to the road. I sprinted and slid over and over, and tried to make each slide longer than the last. I felt unbeatable, heroic, free. Strong limbs and young heart still skilled at suppression. On one of the approaches, without warning, my knees buckled and I slammed into the ice. I knew I hadn't lost my footing because the sagging began at my neck and accordioned downward along my back to my knees. I blacked out.

"I'm sorry, Peter, I'm sorry," I heard Richard crooning as if in an echo chamber. I didn't answer, just lay there wondering what had happened. His face hovered uncomfortably close, magnified, and his forehead was wrinkled.

"You're hurt! You shouldn't have run in front of where I was throwing," he said, stroking my neck and cheeks. He wiped the hair out of my eyes.

So, it was a rock. He showed it to me. The size of an onion. My scalp felt slushy when I groped to determine the damage. Richard urged me to hurry and though I hated the idea of getting up, I managed to stand, and then arm in arm we stumbled home. He offered to help me inside but my fears had subsided and I reassured him that I'd be all right. Before stepping inside, I took off my black Ivy League jacket, my pride and joy, and saw that blood soaked my white t-shirt. It seeped down in a red crescent from my left shoulder to below my right armpit.

As I walked down the hall I poked my head into all the rooms. My mother sat in her bedroom by her Singer machine, back toward me, feet pumping the pedals slowly. Metal things in front of her whirred and clicked like knives and forks.

"Mom," I called from the doorway, "look!"

She turned and I gave her just a second to absorb the picture. I crossed my eyes, rolled them up into my head, and pitched forward face down. Smoothly, without bringing my hands up to break the fall until the last instant. Every kid practises fainting but I guess this was altogether too real and I wasn't prepared for her reaction. She screamed three or four times, quick gusts as if she had too much air in her lungs and couldn't expel it efficiently. Like Joan Sutherland's breathing exercises. It was a mean trick and I was instantly ashamed. I'd only wanted to be the long-suffering hero coming home.

After supper two neighbourhood boys stopped by.

"Wha ja doin? Want to come along?" asked Harold. He was tall, slow, with a standing wave that Carl Smith would have envied. An obvious leader who didn't say much himself because the other kid with him would always explain his ideas for him.

"Harold's got sixty cents," James breathed. "He swiped it from his piggy bank." He needn't have whispered, there was no one else around. And Harold smiled because he was the kid with the money. I longed to go, as much for the company as for the treats. They were both a year older than I was and up until grade nine, when the three of us were finally at the same level in school, they never included me in their plans. Like the clubhouse they built in an abandoned granary (I remember the half bottle of green, enticing Creme de Menthe warming on the ancient Franklin there one winter evening). Or fixing that old Prefix they bought for $10.00 that they raged around the pasture on. And plank surfing on the dugout. They'd sit on a two-by-twelve tied to the bumper of Harold's brother's, Alden's, avocado '53 De Soto. When the De Soto really got cruising and the slack in the line gave out, they'd have a three-second ride and then about two seconds to dive off before the plank cavorted up out of the far side.

"You're not going anywhere today," my mother said, biting off a thread, glancing up at me out of the tops of her eyes.

"Please, Mom, let me go!" I pleaded, though I knew from the tone of her voice there was no point asking.

"No! Not today."

"Why not?"

"Because I said so. And that's final!" She flipped the flywheel at the side of the machine a couple of times to get it going.

So I watched at the road while the other two loped off toward town. I assumed that was what mothers were for.

Denying their sons' desires. Justifying their sons' imaginations. It only dawned on me much later that sons are supposed
to disobey their mothers if they want to grow up healthy.

Healthy, not wise. There's a difference. Earning the right
to wear the penis erect through disobedience. Stealing apples
at six, telling dirty jokes at ten, and eventually maybe cruis-
ing the villages for pick-ups with an older brother who already
has his driver's licence. Richard, for instance, knew the ropes
at fifteen. Knew how brassieres were fastened. His brother
let him tag along occasionally and on one trip, to Altbergthal
I think it was, a few miles from where I lived, they picked up
a village girl who let them have their way. Once parked,
Richard leaned over the front seat and watched Gordon
unbutton her blouse. After a while, he even reached out and
palmed one of her breasts. I admired his audacity and
equated my own dismal inexperience in that area with
stupidity. How was I to understand my mother's fear of Eros?

I was elated when Harold and James promised to bring
me back whatever I ordered. I imagined the rows of high
shelves behind the counter of J.A. Fehr's store with its
inspiring assortment of candies and debated what I could
realistically ask for. J.A. Fehr sounded like the kind of name
that should have had 'and Sons' added, but Fehr only had
daughters. His store was the kids' favourite because farmers
and the chronically unemployed loafed there in overalls and
flannel shirts, smoking and talking, silent when children
walked in as if they had nothing more interesting to occupy
them than such innocence. And because old Mr. Fehr asked
you riddles or challenged you to do something outrageous like
sing a verse of "God Rest Ye Merry Gentlemen" in April or spit
into a cup five feet away on the coal-coloured floor. If you had
the nerve it took he'd throw in an extra five cents' worth of
toffee or licorice rope or sometimes a few Black Cat singles if
you looked over fourteen.

"How much do you want to spend on me?" I tenored, scared that their generosity was a trick. "Would some nigger balls and some Topps cards be too much?"

"No problem. But you gotta wait right here or you don't get nothing," James warned. I nodded too vigorously. Before they disappeared from sight, they turned and pointed and I waved back at them.

What a treasure I'd stumbled on. This was as good as Trixie Belden discovering her aunt's lost diamond brooch under Gypsy Jim's caravan. Like Philip in *The Castle of Adventure* realizing that it was Kiki ordering him to wipe his nose. This is how Chet Morgan must have felt having the Hardy Boys as friends, fat as he was and not nearly as smart.

But I must have been suspicious. Surely I didn't stand there mindlessly trusting those two as if I'd done something to deserve their kindness.

I waited there till they came back. I was restless but not exactly what you would call bored. Friendship and the lure of treats count for much more with a kid than threats and moralizations. I probably climbed the sugar maple (box alder, really) as a diversion and alternated between standing and sitting by the hydro pole from which I could see down the road all the way to town. When they saw me there they would know I had kept my part of the bargain.

Finally, I did see them. For the longest time they seemed to be in no hurry. The specks didn't grow and I only guessed that it was them. About a quarter of a mile away from me they turned in behind Stobbe's cottonwood shelter-belt and then when they re-emerged they came along more quickly.

"We forgot what you wanted," James called when they were twenty yards away, "so we bought you some Cheesies." I'd never heard of Cheesies before and when I saw them I was doubly disappointed. There was no sugar, no candy, after all, just some puffy yellow things floating in a plastic bag filled with tan liquid. I was uninterested. But, out of courtesy, I reached for the sack that James held out. What could I do? They'd thought about me and brought me something, and I had to show gratitude.

"This is how they come, and there's a certain way you have to eat them," James bellowed. He was puffing from the walk.

"Just drink the liquid first and then eat the Cheesies. The sauce tastes real good. It's the best part," Harold evangelized. Tell-tale stains of an Orange Crush fattened his upper lip.

The bag was open at the top and bulging and difficult to hold, but I managed to drink in a mouthful. I spit it out. Piss! They roared then, each short breathless laugh a geyser after which they focussed on my face to catch any further developments. Each laugh slicing me inside. Don't let them think you're angry. Act as if it could happen to anyone. Oh, you're so stupid. If only they don't tell the others. They knew you'd fall for it. So I forced myself to laugh, too.

Eventually they left, still snickering, though we were good friends now because I was such a good sport, they claimed. I lay in my bunk downstairs for an hour. Until supper. But I wasn't hungry. The chicken and potatoes and corn and even the lemon pie tasted the same, like piss, and I wondered if anything would ever be normal again. I was cursed. I pictured myself forever, for all of what was left of my life, for the whole of what was left of my miserable existence, eating and drinking things that might as well have been dunked in our outhouse.

VIGIL

My father's Watkins district extended thirty miles in every direction from home except south. Gretna north to Morris and Emerson west to Winkler. Six days a week he would restock the Ford station wagon with what had been sold the day before—Watkins Camphor Balm, Watkins Antiseptic Salve, Watkins Medicated Ointment—and disappear for fourteen hours or more. His invitation to me to accompany him one summer day was a reprieve from the lazy bird-hunting, creek-swimming boredom of a month to go till grade eight. That day he was servicing the farms around Kane.

The morning proved to be everything I had hoped for. A Pepsi Cola at the Ford Garage in Rosenfeld, a long drive with a few brief stops where my father tried to collect on unpaid bills, a hamburger in Plum Coulee, and all the mysteries of my father's life happily still to unravel. But then it was afternoon and there wasn't much to do during the hour-long stops around Kane. The tedium of prairie, a feeling that I had by this time of day admitted to myself, was symbolized by the Kane elevator visible through the insect-flecked windshield at almost every stop. Sometimes I could see the Kane Hotel and I wondered what the bad men inside did all day long. The hotel isn't a hotel now and there's no beer available in town. Kane is in fact only a shell of its past. Partly because its farmers retire to the more progressive town of Plum Coulee while the Coulee farmers end up in Winkler.

But what would I have done while I waited? After half an hour cooped up in a car a kid has already tried everything twice. Rapping the crack in the windshield with the heel of his hand, counting chickens, opening the door and growling at the dog peeing on the tire and slamming it terrified when it turns to bark, drawing and erasing names, swear words and pictures in the dust on the dashboard till there are no more dusty spaces left.

The possibilities are endless, but of some things I have a clear memory. The dogs ruled out a walk around the yard so I had to be content with what could be done in the car. I opened the little white metal caps on medicines and took small tastes, I sniffed ointments, and I pocketed a roll or two of Wintergreen candies that I'd been warned not to touch. A dusty white chicken sidled around the edge of the house and walked into the middle of the yard where it stood huddled against the wind, hackles fluttering. I rubbed my lips slowly back and forth along the coolness of the door handle until it was too warm to feel good. From underneath the extra receipt book and the New Testament in the glove compartment I dug out the Manitoba Highways map and traced the rural roads we'd have to take to get home.

So why was I so excited all of a sudden? Patsy Cline singing "I Fall to Pieces" on the CKY station I was secretly listening to? Did the young dog try to mount the old one? Was it there that I saw the girl in shorts cross from the hidden back door of the house to the barn, pause and cock her head as if listening, and then step inside? Whatever it was, the disturbance began to grow between my legs. It angered me and guilt twisted my stomach tighter than a knot in a bursting garden hose. After a few minutes of *de facto* resistance, I furtively helped it along, frightened that I wouldn't finish before my father came out of the house. Frightened that a farm boy's grinning face would appear at the car window out of nowhere. When I was done and the Kleenex box was restored to its place under the driver's seat, I prayed that God would forgive me and strengthen me, and then I took up my vigil again.

A FEW GREEN BRANCHES IN SPRING

Cottonwoods guarded neighbour Stobbe's house (and they still do though the occupants have changed and my parents have snuck off to B.C. long ago). The trees were sky-high, fat and close together like a row of confessional booths with narrow doors. I couldn't have squeezed between some of them. Not that I would have wanted to. It would have meant stepping into a front yard crowded with lilacs. Old lilacs, tangled like stolen government fish nets, dead, with only a few green branches in spring, branches that didn't flower, that never smelled of lavender.

Sometimes during the day I'd stand on the road in front of their house, the first house in a line of twenty in our village, and soak in the oldness of the yard. The old yellow clapboard house, the barn, sun-dyed grey and pink, with its once-white X on the double doors, the orchard of Trail and baking apple trees that looked more like a wilderness than a garden and was so overgrown that there was no point sneaking in there to look for windfall, and further back in the pasture, which had been cowless for at least ten years, the three old cars that had been slowly driven to death by Mr. Stobbe, two black ones and one red, abandoned on their bellies in the long grass.

I'd sometimes stand and gawk during the day, but not after dark. At night, if I had to walk past there, say after trumpet practice at the Parkside School or after Young People's at the Bergthaler church, I'd run the gauntlet of the trees. The whole personality of the yard stared out at me then from behind poplar bars. Even if there was no wind down on the ground, especially if there was no wind, the thick leaves high up there swished like the pantlegs of an army of fat men or hissed like the host of Milton's snakes. I'd hear them already a quarter of a mile away. Gossiping, whispering, teasing.

Daniel was what was wrong with that place. How can someone, a single being, someone you never see except once or twice a year, corrupt an otherwise normal household? Like termites. The house looks reasonably good from the outside. I suppose that's not so odd, really; each haunted house has its *spiritus mundi*. We conjure up sly and elusive occupants for certain houses that have that gothic feel about them, hags who slink around at night, whom no one can actually remember talking to. They don't delight in things, because that would make them obviously sentimental, but casually cook up meals every day that require bits and pieces of dogs and cats. These are women whose neighbours' cats and dogs go missing, who have no mailbox at the local post office and who never get any letters anyway, who grow older than ravens.

But what was wrong with Daniel's house was not only imagined. It had five people in it, they kept a garden and, though he had retired a bit too early for my father's sense of what was right and bucked the system by driving around in a 1936 Ford Woody that I'd still like to get my hands on, old Mr. Stobbe was friendlier than probably any other grown-up around there. He loved kids. Would do anything for them that didn't cost money. Probably because he was one of those old-timers who'd never thought of the world in terms of currency.

I still miss him. He died in 1975 of lung cancer. Obviously it was all those years of smoking Old Chum rollies. He'd save up the butts in his left-hand shirt pocket until he had enough to roll a new one. I imagine there were probably still a few shreds of tobacco in the last cigarette he smoked left over from one he rolled, say, in 1932. The middle and the lit end of his cigarettes were fatter than the mouth end. He didn't roll them miserly thin like Mary Jane Martins's father, who hated kids. Hated them maybe because he had a pretty daughter.

But Mrs. Stobbe. Now there was another matter. Wouldn't talk to you. Had nothing to do with neighbours. Was it her ennui that had hardened their pew? Something there between the mother and son? Maybe the son isn't Stobbe's? A trip to Regina when she's, oh, twenty-five, for medical reasons? A few timid nights with the chiropractor she's gone to see about a recurring chest pain? Or, since Daniel's the youngest child, possibly at first a coat-of-many-colours reluctance to share him with anyone else?

I'm fourteen, standing on Stobbe's porch with Richard. Richard is a year younger and he lives at the other end of the village on a farm which his brothers run because his father has been dead for five years. We spend our summers bored together. We kill time hunting frogs with slingshots, we make wine from stolen preserves, we scour the fields for corncobs big enough to make new pipes from. There's a swallow's nest in the corner to the left where the porch roof meets the house and baby birds are chirping in it. The roof keeps out the sun and its shadow cools our backs. A framed picture of Christ holding a lamb sits on the wide window ledge on this side of the blind. The only colour left in it is a hint of blue in Christ's mantle. We knock and wait. They always keep the blinds closed and the inside of the house is black. It dawns on us that there is a figure standing by the screen door and suddenly it is cold under the porch roof as if we'd just jumped into Richard's dugout.

"Can we watch TV today?" I ask as politely as possible because they don't always let us come in and they have the only TV in the village. No answer. The door begins to open. We think it's Mr. Stobbe. Someone runs up from somewhere further inside the house. We hear Daniel's name, a scuffle and a whisper which we can't make out but which sounds like, What are you doing here! And, I want to, I want to, I want to. The door closes and opens again a few moments later.

"No. Not today." It's Mrs. Stobbe. "Mr. Stobbe isn't home," she says, slamming the screen door. "You can come back some other time. Maybe tonight, for 'Route 66'." She stands there. I presume she's watching us as we back down the porch steps, though I can't make out her face. The birds in the nest have stopped singing.

What is it about the deformed that makes us want to manipulate them? It's not as if they were plasticine. Do they threaten us? We control them, keep them conspicuous by hiding them so that when they come out in public everyone thinks, he's coming out now, I wonder why? Probably snuck out. Oh look, Jem, Boo's going into the outhouse. Mrs. Yepanchin, my dear, I think that that idiot is actually in love with your Aglaya! Our hiding them is deliberate self-exposure. Sitting naked in church because life doesn't give most of us many chances to do that. Life makes us pretend we are reasonable, clean, cute, smart, well built. Images of the numinous. So our crookedness in hiding the crooked is a relief from secrecy. A public confession.

I've never seen Daniel close up. Only across the garden fence that separates our yards. I've got a tree-house in one of the alders that grow on the north border between our properties. Though he usually waits till it's dark to go out, and I've heard his newspaper rustling close by at times, occasionally I see him from up there as he stumbles around their yard. He uses the outhouse in summer and that's where he usually goes first, the crab grass farther away from the house knee-high on his old Co-op green overalls, the cow stink that he must be smelling as he approaches the side of the barn where the manure is piled, fluffing about him, getting in his eyes and under his tongue. Then he goes into the garden toward the apple trees and after that he walks behind the barn to where the old cars are, holding down the barbed wire with one hand as he crosses the fence that has no cows to keep in, and adjusting his face-cover with the other. He sits in the cars in spring when the sun is hot through the glass.

He can't see me. The newspaper that he holds in front of his face is tilted away from him at the bottom so he can see his feet but not the sky. I can see the top of his head. It has a small bald spot and his hair is part black and part grey. There are no rings on the fingers that curl around the edge of the paper. The fingers are white and thin. Not like his father's red stubby ones with the dirty nails and one nail that's black from some accident, probably with a hammer or a bicycle wrench.

His father fixes our bikes if we ask him. He does it for free. He's good to us kids. He lets us smoke in his house when we visit him. When we are smoking in his living-room, Daniel is always upstairs.

What did he do there all those years in his bedroom upstairs? Wait to die? Plan bank robberies like Richard and I did the summer we were sixteen? Invent things? I sometimes heard people say he was a genius. A mechanical wizard.

You should see the great contraptions up in his room. A toy train that he can switch on from his bed without getting up and that runs up over his furniture and under his bed and it has real bridges and signal lights and level crossings and there's a church and a hotel and a farm and barn and everything. He's invented a way of getting food upstairs without having to go down for it.

Did he read a lot? The newspaper, maybe? Just grab what was handy to cover his face when he went outside? The *Mennonite Reporter*? Doubtful. He didn't attend church so no need to impress the people who did. *Harper's*? Maybe he was bright enough. Maybe he hid his face from a practical world he was sure he understood but was afraid didn't understand him.

My mother on Daniel. She would deny this now, or at least would tell a different story because she's had a lot of years to think now that she's not distracted by a houseful of kids. She's wise now, she was busy before. Don't go over there when Daniel is in the yard. Mrs. Stobbe wouldn't want you there. Daniel needs his privacy. He has to have a chance to exercise without kids hanging around him. He doesn't want to meet anyone. I asked Erma once—Mrs. Stobbe's name is Erma— what was the matter with him. Shouldn't he be going to school? And she said that he thought he was ugly. That the school kids had teased him when he first started and then they kept him home so he wouldn't feel bad.

I saw him once. I was in their kitchen inviting her to Sewing Circle and he came down from upstairs and into the room and he wasn't wearing a newspaper. He's not ugly! Not really. Oh, his face has some funny spots as if he burned it sometime—maybe he fell in the boiling water like your cousin Arnold—and his mouth is a little crooked, but that's all. Mrs. Stobbe quickly stepped in front of him so I couldn't see and sent him back upstairs. Well, anyway, it's too late for him now.

Muriel Ginter on Daniel. I was coming home from school and I had to go to the bathroom sooo bad. I just couldn't wait. Don't laugh! I would have peed my panties! And I ran to their outhouse. I opened the door and there he was. Right there. Sitting on the hole looking at me. He right away put his hands up over his face. Oh, I was so scared! I mean, you know! I could see . . . everything!

God watches Daniel's prayer sneak up through the ancient poplar planking of the attic and spiral like mist skyward above the TV antenna, rise through the leaves of the cottonwoods, mix with all the other prayers of the village, of Altwelt, of Manitoba, of Canada, and finally twist itself into the rope of the prayers of the whole world. God, make me whole! Make me the same as everyone! I am so tired, being alone, of being in my room with my toy train and of hiding, and of people, and of Mom and of Dad and of me, and of me, and of me.

RED AND WHITE

As he passed Widow Sawatsky's white pig barn and its ammonia pumped in through the Volkswagen's open window, Thomas remembered that in a few minutes he'd be facing his mother and he reconciled himself to the fact that life as he had envisioned it was over. He winched away at the window handle with the knob missing and raised his bucket seat into a more upright position. What was done was done. There was no turning back. He'd have to go on somehow but his self-worth, his status, his general dependability as a Christian, were finished. What would Alveira be thinking right now? How could he have been so stupid? He swerved to avoid a case of empty beer bottles. The seat collapsed back into the recline position and dust billowed up from its tan corduroy upholstery.

Thomas tore down Lovers' Lane. The half mile of cotton-woods that bordered the road and screened it from the town blurred by at the edge of his thoughts. A town crew had raked the leaves. They were the pale yellow of dried marigolds and lay heaped around the bases of the trunks like crumpled sundresses. Snow salted the air and powdered the leaves. The trees' branches, bare so you couldn't tell which ones were dead or alive, twisted upwards toward a heavy tick of clouds. When he pulled away from the stop sign onto Main he stayed in first gear and puttered along. There was no rush getting home.

Except for a few corner stores and garages that hardly counted, all of Altwelt's businesses were lined up along Main. As if they'd come out to watch him. Or not. They seemed to glower, seemed like friends who'd turned their backs on him. Even the few people who were on the street didn't notice him.

He hadn't been home enough. He'd been too busy with Introductory Old and New Testament, student elections, and auditions and practices for the Christmas Oratorio. All the sacrifices he'd made. The hot rods he hadn't built, the beer and wine he hadn't touched, the girls he hadn't dated in recognition of St. Paul's wisdom, the church choir he'd helped direct from grade eleven on and even for a year after high school when he worked for the *Altwelt Mirror*, the evangelical street meetings he'd stood through when you couldn't find another town kid his age in the crowd. On the critical periphery yes but not in the audience. And the street meeting testimonies of the Free Church types he'd felt guilty being ashamed of and had always smiled and nodded at in show of support. How soon they forgot. Where was the gratitude they'd heaped on him then?

The blacksmith's shop, Arne's, squatted between the brick and brass Bank of Montreal and Eleanor's Ladies' Fashions. It was a white wooden hut the size of a large granary with double doors held open by long, rusted, iron carriage axles. Outside of Sunday, its doors were never closed except on the coldest days when Arne didn't bother showing up at all. Even now with the snow flying they yawned, too tired to close. It was impossible to see what was inside unless you actually stepped into the building. A dirt floor and dirt and soot from the forge, probably still left over from horseshoeing days, blackened the interior. You couldn't tell if Arne was there unless you stepped inside. He was inevitably as black as the room itself.

Arne liked his beer. His gut hung over his black belt and jiggled like a water-filled condom. His shirt wasn't long enough and dirt and grease and hair made his stomach as black as the thighs of his overalls. Such people bothered Thomas. People whose appearance more than hinted at their sinfulness. Indians who came every spring to weed beets for farmers who simply couldn't convince whites that the job was respectable. He knew what they were like. For four months every summer they subsisted here in old granaries like they'd lived in their tents or shacks in Roseau or Grand Rapids or Sandy Bay with clutter and mess, dressed in filthy clothes, charity clothes. What was the matter with them? Decent folk wouldn't do that, not if there was anything they could possibly do to help it. They weren't even smart about their clothes. Thomas would see them suddenly with new dark blue jeans or new polished shoes on the beetfield and it'd surprise him like stepping in a fresh cow-patty. They begged around town for money (if you gave them food you'd find it again in the ditch a few hundred yards up the road). And they roared around when they should have been working, in rust buckets they'd bought drunk at inflated prices at Wiens's Ford Mercury or West End Pontiac, which stocked up on beaters at this time of the year. They spent all their earnings at the Altwelt Beer Parlour, and then disappeared till next year.

Friedensruh Fronz, who pedalled around Carman and Morden and Gnadenthal and Reinland and New Horst on a bicycle with a sack over his shoulder for collecting beer bottles. You'd see him any month of the year with that bike.

Run into him five miles from town pushing it along a foot-deep car tire rut in the snow. He'd stop and pull his bicycle aside and stand and watch you for half a mile before you'd got to him and half a mile after you'd passed.

The lipsticked and rouged and perfumed women and bleary-eyed men who hung around the Elks' Hall Saturday night. Dance night, show night. At eighteen, he'd never seen a movie, never stepped on a dance floor.

The beer parlour door opened and Arne stepped out, unsteady. A few years back, fired up into an ecstasy of guilt by a two-night Brunk tent revival at the fairgrounds, Thomas had confronted Arne right there on those same steps. You've got to make use of every opportunity to witness for the Lord, Brunk's assistant had said in the room at the back of the tent to those who'd stayed behind after the first meeting. You mustn't be ashamed of making your Christianity public. Fair enough, but it had been easier being a witness than an effective witness.

"Aren't you worried about your salvation?" he'd blurted to Arne. He'd looked over his shoulder first. This needn't take long, he'd thought. The street was empty. Not a car or person in sight. In the distance, a dust eddy sneaked out of Fourth beside the Co-op store, worried about on Main for a second, and disappeared behind the orange Pool elevator. The hitching rail by the coal shed next to the tracks faded as the dust devil passed.

"What?" Arne said. He looked over his shoulder and back at Thomas. The step wasn't wide enough and he reached for the iron railing and held on with both hands. His eyes narrowed and he bent his head forward. Tufts of black hair curved out of his nose. His head lifted up, dipped down, in time with his breathing. The smell of cigarette smoke and beer hit Thomas and he stepped back half balanced.

"What're you talkin' about?" Arne said, leaning away from

Thomas into the railing and groping for the package of cigarettes in a brown shirt pocket edged with grease. A fat man in dirty, wide suspenders stepped out of the parlour, blinked in the fresh light, looked at both of them as if he couldn't quite figure out what conference would finally after all these years have to be held right there on the front steps of the pub, and elbowed his way past, farting at every step like a horse pulling a plow.

"What if you die today?" Thomas said, when the fat man was far enough away. "Where do you think you'd end up? God loves us all and he can help us with any problems we have. He forgives us our blackest sins," he said, looking at Arne's mouth but not his eyes. Arne's lips, wet, the texture and pinkness of a pig's snout, were ringed with blackheads visible despite the soot because he'd been licking them. An old picture of Billy Graham filled Thomas's head. Bible in one hand, hair combed to perfection, Brylcreem shine, back edge cut razor neat, standing before a crowd of fifty thousand, straight as a telephone pole, each short sentence a miracle, pausing for four or five seconds to let it sink in.

"Who the hell are you?" Arne asked, his hand still searching for his pocket.

Thomas climbed up another step. "Thomas Regier," he said, but Arne's eyes looked blank. "Henry Regier's son. The Watkins man."

Arne found his pocket, fiddled with the package till his black fingers came up with a cigarette, and stared at him while he lit it. His eyes were laughing. "Never seen you," he said.

"We were in your place a few weeks ago," Thomas said. "With the Lawn Boy." Arne shook his head and took a long slow drag. The lit end of the cigarette forged an inch-long ember. Arne turned and started down the step, the white cigarette dangling from his thick, black fingers.

"You welded a new handle," Thomas said to his back.

"Never heard of you," Arne said without looking back when he reached the sidewalk.

"You must know my dad," Thomas called after him. But Arne didn't answer and Thomas watched him till he disappeared, trailing a blue swirl of smoke like incense from a censer, through the double doors of his shop.

There was the Bank of Montreal, which Thomas had never seen from the inside because he and his father did all their banking at the credit union. The Co-operative Consumers building, hardware and grocery, cracked, chipped, peeling white stucco and siding, gangly with too many sections added on that snaked into the nooks and crannies beside and behind other stores. The Western Shoe Repair shop, with windows that looked like they'd never been washed, probably because it made less money than any other business in town and the owner was too busy with ten- and twenty-five-cent jobs to actually take a break and do some cleaning. Or he'd become indifferent, Yertle the turtle at the bottom of the pile, the humble not needing to be clean.

Mrs. Caryluk's, at one time the old town office, was one of two quarried stone buildings in Altwelt. The bottom floor had been a dress shop a few years ago, Alice's, until Alice went back to Winnipeg where she'd come from. Alice was different from other town women. Prettier, redder, more graceful. Farmers, with their overalls and barn boots, and their wives didn't come into her shop. It stood empty now but Mrs. Caryluk still used only the second floor.

Thomas had worked for her for a few months when he was fifteen. She'd given James Ginter fifty cents to dust her throw rugs on Saturdays and James had given him twenty-five cents to help him. They'd carried the rugs downstairs—some of them weighed a hundred pounds—hung them on the washline in the back yard and beat away at them with broom handles. If it hadn't been for the money Thomas wouldn't have been seen with James. He's lazy, like his dad, Thomas had thought, and he'd worried that James was trying to get into his good graces now so that he could play a trick on him later. There was the time James and his older brother and his older brother's friend had tried to force him to renounce God. To say he wasn't a Christian. If you smoke a cigarette right now we'll know, they'd said. He'd smiled at them as kind as he could, though inside he'd been jack-rabbit scared, and quoted John 3:16: "For God so loved the world that he sent his only begotten son that whosoever believeth on him shall not perish but have everlasting life." Not perish, eh, they'd said, and dunked his head in the rain barrel behind Ginter's cow barn, and held it there. Four times they'd done it and after each time they'd given him another chance. The last time he'd been sure he'd drown. Held his breath as long as he could and then his air had bubbled out and he'd sucked water deep into his lungs. Now maybe I'll meet Jesus, he'd thought. When they'd finally pulled his head back, he'd collapsed at their feet and they'd run off.

James was the second youngest of eleven kids. His mouth never seemed to quit. But he never talked about his parents. His father had once been a farmer, though as long as Thomas could remember he hadn't had a job. In fact, Thomas had never seen him in the yard. With all that time on his hands the father could have at least painted the house, Thomas thought. It was one of two in the village which didn't have a speck of paint on them. The house and the chicken shed and the cow barn and the outhouse were grey in sunlight and black in rain. Their pigsty had been empty for years. By fall it was filled with pigweed which stuck up like cornstalks three feet above the highest board on the fence. None of the outbuildings except the outhouse was used for anything. There wasn't a cow to milk and there were no chickens to feed.

The grass in their yard had never been cut. Two old cars and parts of others—motors, fenders, wheels—stacked in a sort of row, showed where the barbed-wire fence had once separated their yard from their neighbour's.

Thomas thought of James's sister, Muriel. How from a particular day on he'd avoided her. The Ginters had a strawberry patch and it was the only sign of ambition in the yard. Because Thomas's father drove Mrs. Ginter to church every Sunday she offered them free strawberries every spring. One day Thomas's mother sent him over with two wine-grape baskets and after he'd picked for a while, Muriel appeared with a small pail and began picking too, squatting on her haunches across the row from him. She chattered as she picked, but he couldn't speak. He nodded politely or answered her questions with a word or two because she was a year older. He was embarrassed, worried he'd be seen.

Muriel prattled on about how she liked strawberries more than anything, about hating her grade ten teacher, about having kissed Brian Stobbe under the railway bridge. She was wearing a dress and had it hiked up just above her knees. The flash of her white legs, shifting as she leaned to pick here and there, lured him. He shouldn't be looking, he thought, and decided to keep his eyes down. But he couldn't resist and finally pretended to be searching for berries closer to her feet. While he rummaged in among the strawberry leaves with his hands, bent forward so Muriel wouldn't be able to see his face, he peeked up at her shins. Her knees were parted the width of a hand, but as he watched they spread, slowly, slowly, wider. He forgot she might see him looking. Her skirt inched toward her waist. Sunlight shone on more and more of her thighs until nothing was hidden. She wasn't wearing anything underneath and he saw the black hair and pink, wet folds of skin where her thighs met. He jerked up his head. She stared at him with a set smile, then reached down and slithered her skirt back over her knees, first one side and then the other. He picked up his almost empty basket and ran. He didn't tell his mother.

He drove by Mrs. Bringer's corner store. It was a tall, faded yellow building that had looked shabby ever since he'd first seen it. I never liked going in there, he thought. You always expected something, a crippled, fat daughter maybe, to crawl out of the room at the back and haul herself up there beside her mother and peer over the countertop at you. Or a little man with white hair, black shirt and black pants, in morning slippers, shuffling into the light with a plate of fried potatoes and smoked ham for Mrs. Bringer.

It was the oldest building in town as far as he knew. The wooden shiplap crumbled when you pressed your hand or fingers against it. Tens of thousands of kids from the west end of town on their way to the Altwelt Elementary School had picked at the rotting wood. On the south side, till six feet above the ground, the building looked especially ragged. Thomas had kept coming to this store when he had money to spend. He'd never seen a light on inside. The only illumination came from the narrow front window, dirty with dust, through which light filtered, sifted in, reluctant.

Mrs. Bringer stood behind the counter. Always in the same spot. Never anywhere else. She was quiet, almost mute, not starved for conversation, though she was polite and didn't make you feel you should leave. Nobody else ever seemed to be in the store. Just the woman, standing, watching, as if she'd been waiting for a week or two for you to ask for nigger babies or spearmint gum.

And as the light outside faded, the back of the inside of the store became invisible, black, and you could make out only the things on the unpainted shelves closest to the window. Dusty blue and white china cups and figures, glass jars with red and yellow beads and old thread and faded candy, a mousetrap with a piece of bread in it, and higher up, close to the ceiling, a row of plaster of Paris girl dolls in flounces and lace. Fly-paper packed with black bodies hung above the cash register. The store didn't have hours. Its door was never locked. You just didn't open it when you thought it would be too dark to see what you'd come to buy.

But no one ever did come out of the back, Thomas thought. Maybe no one else lived there. Maybe she was a Communist or an NDP. Maybe she was a lesbian and had to live alone. Who knew what persecution she'd suffered? Maybe she never wanted to spend her life selling junk in a small Manitoba town. What if she'd had high hopes of studying at a university and just hadn't had the money and so she started a business to save little by little till she could afford her dream? But no one seemed to want her stuff and she couldn't save a dollar and became less and less active until, with people and life itself not empathizing, she wanted to do nothing more than stand in one spot day after day behind her counter? Uninterested in her goods and the people who sometimes bought them. Maybe she'd been the war bride of one of those Mennonites who'd refused to be conscientious objectors and, instead of planting trees in Nanaimo as his grandfather had done, or cooking for a gang of road clearers on the Veder in the Fraser Valley like his Uncle Reuben, actually ended up in England training and drinking and whoring and then fighting on the front lines against the Desert Fox.

He would have to marry Alveira now, he thought. A kid came out of the pool hall, looking back over his shoulder, and ran across the street in front of him and he had to slam on the brakes. He was tempted to honk but decided against it. He'd been speeding up again. That's one of those Heinrichses, he thought. You could tell them by their thin beak noses and turnip-shaped heads. The diameter of their skulls was only

half as wide at their chins as at their foreheads. Probably
Bernie Heinrichs's brother. Bernie'd had to get married to a
girl from Letellier when he was in grade twelve. He'd been
one of the tough kids. Definitely not a Christian. Smoked,
went to dances in Gretna and Emerson and Cavalier, wasted
a lot of time in the pool hall, always had girls hanging around
him. And he was separated already.

What a waste to get married now, Thomas thought. How
many guys, with his potential, had been sincerely concerned
about the idea of salvation? About the afterlife? Not many.
Maybe none. Not even the other Bible School students, really.
He'd begun to see in the last few years that his whole dream
of becoming an evangelist was not where the answers to the
salvation problem lay for him. He'd find the answers in books,
in systematic theology. In the writings of Buber, Tillich, the
Niebuhr brothers, Bonhoeffer and those others that he'd
already begun to read at CMBC.

He'd felt special. In some way he'd been chosen, anxieties
and paranoias included, to accomplish something unique for
God. In the area of epistemology, he'd thought when he'd first
heard that word. To further man's actual understanding of
the divine. Through preaching and church work, yes, but
more through pure living. By being holy and diligent so he
could be a proper receptacle for God's will and spirit. Like
Paul. But that dream was shot now.

Thomas stopped for gas at the Esso station on the corner
where the village road began. Half a mile from home. Half a
mile from confession. The building's old plaster was still as
white as if it were new but chunks of it had broken away along
the foundation. The red facia board had bled and discoloured
the stucco all along under the flat roof. Snow half-filled the
pot-holes in the heavy traffic areas close to the gas bowsers.
He waited in the car for a while and then went in and stood
at the restaurant counter. Still no one. He could hear voices.

They were probably too lazy to get up from the couch in the living-room at the back, sitting there like that group of freshmen in the student lounge who never studied and then asked for your notes.

Thomas studied the rows of cigarette packages in the shelves behind the cash register. He knew them by their reds and blues and whites, not by their brand names, and he had a sudden urge to buy a pack. Stick it up in the visor above his head like the farm kids. But he thought about what Brunk had said, though he knew it was rather silly, about smokers who would have the added pain of a cigarette burning between their lips in hell forever. Prometheus but with nobody to save him. Not that he was convinced about hell. He was intellectually ambivalent. But then, being convinced had almost no connection, ever, with what he felt or did.

There was no point in putting it off. When he drove into the yard and parked his Volkswagen on the gravel beside the cement driveway so that his father could park the Oldsmobile in its regular spot when he came home, Thomas was thinking that maybe he'd just not mention what had happened. Inside the kitchen he smelled the familiar aromas of Saturday cleaning and baking. Waxed floors and double-decker buns in the oven mixed with the strains of the "Back to the Bible" radio program. His mother's red Sunday dress hanging over a chrome kitchen chair beside the ironing board was the same colour as the red cigarette packages at the Esso station.

"Mom," he called. No answer. Snow rustled around the kitchen window. Advertisements for Massey Ferguson seeders from Enns Implements and a sale on wedding dress material from Penner's Dry Goods announced that the Bible program was over. Thomas called again, louder. This time his mother answered from the washroom down the hall.

He stood just outside its closed door. "Mom," he said, and

waited till she answered. "I've got to talk to you." He kept his eyes on the doorknob.

"Thomas! I'm glad you're finally home," she said, her voice sounding muffled. The smells that came up through the cracks under the door made him uncertain whether he should continue. Why didn't they use deodorant spray? It wasn't that expensive.

"Mom, I'm worried. I've got to tell you something," he said, louder than he would have had to if there'd been an opening of some sort in the door, he thought, or above it like in some of the older houses. His stomach churned as if he'd drunk too much apple juice and for a second he felt the urge to get down on his knees. "It's very hard for me," he said, "and I know it will be hard for you, too. I just need to get it off my chest." The area around his heart ached and his lungs were tight and raw as if he'd just smoked and inhaled a whole package of cigarettes.

"Mom," and tears began to drop on the wrist that he held under his nose, "I think I've made Alveira pregnant." Things were very still. From outside he heard the faint coo of a mourning dove. Then inside the bathroom cotton whispered, elastic snapped and the toilet flushed.

She was a heavy woman, used to pork and cream, slow-walking, preoccupied with day-dreams. Discontent. Later, at age sixty, when her kids were finally out of the house, she would take up painting and become a fairly popular local artist, painting people's homesteads and scenic landscapes from photographs. She walked to where Thomas had found a seat in a chair in the kitchen, wiping her hands on the sides of her dress.

"Thomas," she whispered, "what are you saying?" Her eyes were wide, staring at his without wavering, as fixed as the picture of the little girl on the Co-op calendar behind her. A girl in a short dress and pretty bare legs with one bare arm around the long white neck of a goose and the other holding a Red Ridinghood wicker basket. He turned away.

"I've had a hard time living with this," he said. "The other day, in the music practice room, I kissed Alveira, and . . . she was sitting there playing the piano and she looked so pretty. I was just standing close to her and all of a sudden I kissed her, and then . . . ." He bent down and whispered in her ear.

The flushing in the bathroom stopped with a chunk as the water cock closed the valve. Everything was as still and echoey as the inside of the cement cistern under the garage floor when they cleaned it once a year and he was in it by himself for a while. Sometimes then he imagined how much stiller it'd be if someone didn't know he was down there and covered the hole with its two-hundred-pound cement lid. His mother picked up the red dress and examined a seam in the neckline. "You did, did you?" she said after a while, the crow's-feet at her eyes deepening. "You did that with Alveira?" When Thomas nodded she sat down on a chair, crumpled the dress between both hands and started laughing. She laughed and laughed until she was short of breath.

THE RETARDED DYCKS

Brian was the oldest and the only one of the retarded Dycks who wasn't retarded. His five brothers and one sister didn't have the quick childish smile of Down's syndrome or the low foreheads but they had some odd traits which you couldn't find in textbooks. Their eyes were too far apart and sluggish, they had large, flat, puffy noses, and their heads shivered and waggled so that while they were looking at something the shaking threw off their concentration and they latched on to the next object that drifted into view. The parents were only a little better off. They'd been just bright enough in 1947 to be given a marriage licence and to set up house. Things like that weren't controlled then the way they are now.

Without Brian I don't know what those kids would have done. Got lost in the fields of corn that some of the fathers made their kids grow on the land adjacent to the village to sell later in roadside stands as a way of teaching them good business sense. Or they'd have wound up in Sommerfeld or

Schoenwiese or Reinland, noticed suddenly by the owner of the little brown brick-siding store that sits at the end of each village, standing there in the corner next to the hundred-pound sack of unroasted sunflower seeds to one side of the store-front window, picking their noses, incoherent about how they got there. Or they'd just have wandered around the countryside without food or drink and they'd have been brought home by passing farmers who'd take time out from their busy schedules. Or drowned, probably that. Tried swimming in a dugout because that's what they'd seen other boys doing and they'd want to try it too as soon as they happened to be there alone.

And they'd have fallen asleep on the hot slope of the railway ditch on an early spring afternoon when that is what nature would make anyone do, but not woken till it got cold or till the sun was bright next morning. They'd have stolen cartons of cigarettes at the Co-op store because they'd want to have what they wanted and who would do anything? Who could? They wouldn't be sent to reform school or jail and wouldn't be expected to do community service since they couldn't dig or plant or clean or organize. The police would simply warn them and let them go. And if the police had complained to the parents, what difference would that have made?

So Brian took care of them. They were a close-knit family and when you saw them off their yard—on the road to town, in the post office, or shopping for something at Hi-way Groceteria, say Saturday night after the regular grocery stores were closed—they walked as a group. Brian would lead and the other six would follow, sometimes in single file, sometimes in a hectic bunch.

They were happy and curious. They'd goggle around them with heavy, swaying heads, reach for things, disturb the rhythm of life wherever they happened to be. Hold candy bars at the drugstore counter in their dirty hands and sniff them and pick at the corners of the wrappers until Brian motioned for them to put them back. Stand in front of the receptionist's desk in Dr. Driedger's office, looking at her and smiling when she'd finally stare at them and frown. Hang upside-down by the knees from the mudscraper in front of the post office so people had to squeeze past.

Even so, there was a kind of order about them. A control that made them more careful and obedient, more contained than you would have expected, and it wasn't the result of their parents' discipline. The father and mother were careless themselves and too busy concentrating on walking or driving or paying for something, or whatever they might be doing, to take charge of the kids.

That was Brian's job. But what was odd when you came to think of it, you never heard him instruct them in public. He never said a word, in fact. Not even on the school bus that took us all to town in winter. They'd be on it already, along with twenty-five kids from the villages southeast of town, by the time it stopped at my house. They sat in the front, behind the driver, close to the door. The worst possible spot for them. I was sure then that they would have liked to sit at the back, away from the other kids, alone in their corner with their backs to the wall so they could watch without being watched. Now I think it was more likely us wanting them at the back. Us wanting to be rid of them. Rid of the evidence that we really couldn't keep the Christian fellowship, or maybe that we still had a lifetime of that sort of sacrifice or reminder of failed sacrifice ahead of us.

There were only four of them on the bus because one was too young for school and two were too retarded. Nothing could be done with them in the schools. Those Dycks who attended usually had special corners prepared for them by their teachers, made out of cardboard or draperies or just space, to keep them separate from the others. They'd sit and look around, or draw pictures, or page through picture books, and then just sit some more till the day was done, and then they'd come home by bus again.

One evening in summer when Richard and I and a few of our friends were having coffee in The Harvest Queen, the whole bunch of Dycks came in. The restaurant was long and narrow and had tables on both sides of the aisle. There was barely enough room between the tables to walk through without jiggling people's elbows and spilling drinks. It was a typical summer evening and the place was full of school drop-outs, farm boys from the hinterland in town to check out the girls, especially the ones who stayed out later than ten o'clock.

They filed into the restaurant with Brian in the lead. There was a table at the far back that was empty and they clumped, Charlie Chaplins, through the elbows toward it. The customers at the tables watched them until the Dycks noticed them looking and then turned away. Their clothes were rags. Their shoes were scuffed and big and clumsy. Work boots. The girl stopped at our table and smiled at us like she'd done at every table. Brian pulled at her arm and sat her down. His footsteps had been quiet and his eyes had looked straight ahead. He hadn't smiled.

Like Christ, taking the burdens of the world on his own shoulders. You don't do that and smile. It goes without saying that it's hard. There can't be anything harder. Though with the right attitude toward the calling you might find purpose in it and life would be empty if you suddenly didn't have it to drive you anymore.

We are all retarded kids, ignorant of what's being done for us like the Dyck kids were unaware of what Brian knew and feared and hoped for. But who was Brian doing it for? At least Christ knew what God felt and wanted of him and of us, feared to disappoint him, hoped to be able to die a good death and save the world from the chaos of endless sacrifices to stone gods and golden calves and bring about a reconciliation with God who saw everything and spoke every Sunday morning to Reverend Falk. For Brian there was no release from the knowledge that life is disparate and that we don't know anything that can save us and make it worthwhile other than our simple faith in a *sane* father, someone who has a plan. A cosmic force that is faceless and mysterious. As faceless as the Dyck kids who all looked the same to us and as mysterious as their specific worth on earth. No release except saving his brothers and sister from their vulnerability. From smiling in the face of it all.

So Brian was in charge and he hated it. Loved and hated them. It's an old problem. You look around and see it everywhere. In Altwelt, the butcher at Reimer's Super Dollar hates his wife. They're never apart when he's not at work and you'd swear they were inseparable. She's in the car outside the hotel when he goes in to buy a case of beer and she watches every practice and every game his team plays Tuesday nights at the bowling centre. Mary Epp, my neighbour's teenaged daughter, spends a lot of her time on the concrete steps in front of their house summer evenings. She's sixteen and not allowed to date. She's put out, bound to be. Every girl whose mother won't let her grow up hates and loves her parents. Larry Friesen, who has packed groceries in Enns's Mainstreet Mall for at least five years now and still only earns about minimum wage, hates Victor Enns. Larry's been told he'll be laid off if he's not careful.

We were sitting at the table across from them. Their voices competed and stuttered, went raucous and then apologetic. They didn't worry about manners. When French fries fell on the floor they picked them up and ate them. They would have picked them up out of the gutter and popped them into their mouths without wiping them off if they'd been eating in a hog barn, I thought to myself.

When their ketchup bottle was empty the girl pointed at ours and in the same motion got up and grabbed at it across our table. She was about fifteen and quite pretty. Because she was slim and blonde and pale she stood out from the others who had brown hair and tanned faces and were heavier. Her arms and hands moved with a grace that contrasted with the way she'd walked down the aisle. She tilted the bottle over her plate just as Brian, who sat on the other side of the table, reached across and pinched her soft underarm. Tears grew in her eyes as she turned to look at him. He glared at her for a second, fierce and steady, and then the tension in him died and without saying anything he turned back to his food. After a moment of fiddling in the pile of French fries with her fork she started shovelling them in again, though she didn't use the borrowed ketchup. None of the other Dycks seemed to have noticed any of this. We left the restaurant and I didn't think about them again for a long time.

I've often wondered why Richard and I pulled the stunt we did that fall. It wasn't that I was indifferent to how they felt. I felt sorry for them, I really did. Recognized the ignorance of those of us who looked on as if we were secretly watching lovers or humping dogs or television. I never thought about them when they weren't actually in my sight but when they were I wanted something better for them. Wished they could be normal. Thought that the world had been created unequal and that some of us were a lot better off than others.

In many ways Richard and I shouldn't have been friends. He lived at the far end of the village and I lived at the end closest to town. He was a farmer's kid and my father was a travelling salesman who sold medicines and food colouring and soaps to country women. Richard had 20-20 eyesight and shot the heads off blackbirds from seventy-five yards with his .22 and I was more or less blind, with Coke-bottle glasses, and

I felt guilty about the few robins I'd picked off with a slingshot. It was our last year of high school and life was boring. Nothing we were supposed to do gave us pleasure. Nothing. And on a certain Saturday night, in August I think it was, we were loafing around on the village road, nothing to do.

It was dark and warm. We were in blue jeans and short-sleeved shirts and black and white runners. The lights had gone out in most of the houses. Only Stobbe's and Enns's were still shining way down north along the road. The lights didn't remind us of anything. Not beacons or candles or stars; we weren't in a poetic mood; there'd been nothing for weeks that called for poetry. Not females, fishing, books, or plans to explore the Yukon River.

"Let's throw one of your CVO firecrackers in someone's yard," I said, knowing that Richard would have a specific place in mind. He always had precise ideas about things. For him there was Truth, and uncertainty in the cosmos was not a danger. He thought for a minute before he answered. The cut-clover smell of fresh-mown grass in the ditch filled the air. The slope of the village ditches was steep and it often surprised me to see how the tractors and drivers were slanted when they cut the grass. I had watched them some-times. Followed beside the tractor as it crept along. The cracked rubber wheels with the hacked tread trundled round and round and the old steel retractable cutters sawed away in slow rhythm. Thick, thick, thick, thick, thick, thick, thick, thick. THACK when it hit a rock. Once I'd seen a rabbit jump out of a clump of grass and scurry forward, away from the blades, and then turn and run back into them. The blades snipped off its legs above the knees and it lay there, body jerking as if it thought it was still running, head up watching for the fox, till the farmer got off the tractor and hit it with a jack bar that he took out of the tool-box beside the metal seat.

"There's no one up at the Retarded Dycks," Richard said, watching to see how I'd respond. "We can throw it there. They'll never guess what it was." He was already starting in their direction as if his word were final. His pantlegs swished in the ditch grass as he walked. Why there, I thought. It hadn't dawned on me that he'd choose them. Lots of other places would be better. Widow Hiebert's, for instance, whose apples we stole. She'd caught us a few times when we were younger and told our parents. Or Mr. Brandt who owned Brandt's Cabinets in the village and was rich. Or Mrs. Yoder whose husband had left her and moved to Regina. She yelled at her neighbours and kept a two-hundred-watt bare light-bulb shining over her back yard at night. But not the Dycks, not them! I couldn't tell Richard, though, and we walked together in silence till we came to their house and then we lay down in the ditch so we could size up the place without being seen. Maybe it wouldn't be that bad, I thought. Maybe they'd hardly notice because they were retarded and too dumb to be scared.

There were no lights in their house. A steady breeze blew and shadows of branches rippled over the dirt driveway. Reflected town light showed us the two bedroom windows on this side of the house and there were white curtains in the bedroom next to the driveway. We'd have to hurry if we wanted to get back down that long driveway and into the ditch before the thing went off and someone looked out the window.

We slunk, bent over, to the house. Richard lit the fuse and threw the firecracker down underneath the curtained window and before it hit the grass we were running. We crossed the village road, dove into the ditch, and turned to watch the house. I held my breath, scared. There was reason to be tense. CVO firecrackers aren't dynamite but they pack a wallop. Farmers use them to scare blackbirds out of sunflower fields. Richard and I once threw one into a pool in Buffalo Creek south of Altwelt and afterwards dead fish and frogs floated everywhere belly up.

When the explosion came, the whole west side of the house lit up orange and white for a second. I saw that its weathered siding didn't have a spot of paint, I saw the three little ventilation holes in the old-fashioned storm windows, the Farmall on blocks beside one of the granaries that never held grain, and everything else in their yard as clear as day. There was even a chicken which had escaped roundup, looking around the corner of the house just a few feet from the blast. And then everything was blacker than before. When our eyes adjusted to the darkness I saw that the curtains were still drawn tight. Nothing moved. Nothing had changed. No lights went on inside. It was as if we'd imagined the roar.

"Did you hear glass breaking?" I whispered, holding my head low, my view fuzzy through the tall grass at the edge of the road which the mower had left.

"I'm not sure," Richard said, raising his head a bit higher above the sweet mown grass that smelled like Hyde Park pipe-tobacco mixture or some of those other exotic kinds you can buy these days in Winnipeg at The Pipe Dream or Sherlock Holmes stores. "Can you believe it? No one's even looking out. They must be shit scared," he added, laughing, ducking his head close to mine in conspiracy. He had his hand over his mouth so he wouldn't be heard. I laughed too, though I felt as if I might vomit.

"What do you think they'll figure it was?" I said, hoping they'd turn on their lights. Why weren't they checking out what'd happened? Had we imagined the noise and light? This was all too unnerving. I wanted to leave. The earth wet and cooled my skin where my shirt wasn't long enough to cover my stomach. An ant crawled down the front of my pants.

"I don't know, maybe a gun going off," Richard said, looking at me as if he wasn't quite sure what I meant. He brushed a cobweb off his forehead and turned his eyes back toward the road.

"Look, there they are," he whispered suddenly, pointing without stretching out his arm. A light went on, the curtains wavered and then a head poked through the opened window. It was the girl. Her long yellow hair hung down almost to the windowsill. She had the two halves of the curtain wrapped around her neck but after a minute she let them drop and stood there in clear view. She was naked, the light behind her. Her breasts were in the shadows and her shoulders and the back of her head were lit up. A black shape drifted around the far corner of the house and crawled along the wall till it came even with the window where the girl stood. It stopped. A black arm extended toward the curtains and then the girl pulled them closed.

As soon as he saw the shadow, Richard got up and began to sneak through the ditch and over the yard that separated us from the railway tracks. I was curious about the affair at the house but I didn't want to be left behind so I followed.

"Brian," he said when we stopped. "He's pretty sharp. We're lucky he didn't see us." We were both breathing hard. We lay in the cinders where we'd thrown ourselves down, heads next to the steel rails. The steel tick, tick, ticked as it contracted in the cool night air. "Did you see her?" he added. "Not bad, eh?" I didn't answer him. I knew what he meant, but how could one live with oneself if one thought like that about retarded people? I didn't want to be with Richard anymore just then and after a few minutes I told him I had to go. He headed south down the tracks and I headed north.

School started and the Dyck kids weren't on the bus. Monday morning, a week into the school year, they still weren't there. Surely it couldn't be the firecracker, I reasoned. The blame had to lie with any one of a thousand things that could have happened to them. People staring at them in town in the store. The rags they wore as clothes, and the nice things other school kids had. A change in school policy about allowing retarded kids into normal classrooms. Something like that. Who was to know?

"We should go view the body after four," Richard said as I flopped into the spot he always kept for me beside him on the bus. My heart hammered inside my chest and I was breathing hard. I'd been running. It'd been a bad morning all around. I'd barely started my shredded wheat when my mother yelled that the bus was leaving the neighbours', and it was already moving away from our driveway when I'd come flying out the garage door. Besides all that, I'd realized as I was half-way to the bus that I'd forgotten my lunch bag. Still, I was thankful that the driver had stopped.

"What body?" I said, aware that the section behind the driver was empty again. Richard didn't answer right away and I looked over at him. Our neighbours' giant cottonwoods flipped past the window behind him. Their leaves were just beginning to fall. A few were dropping, and in the silence it seemed I would hear them as they landed. Those that lay on the ground were hidden by tall grass that the Stobbes mowed maybe once a year.

"Brian Dyck's," Richard said, looking out the dirty side window as if he couldn't care less. At least I couldn't make out what he was thinking. He had a toothpick in his fingers and he flick flick flick, flick flick flicked it back and forth along the front of his teeth as if they were a picket fence. "He's dead. The blonde girl found him yesterday hanging in the hay loft, my mom said." Richard glanced at me and then turned back to the window. His black, gleaming hair was combed just so into a high wave in front and a ducktail at the back. There was a dirty grease spot where his wet hair flipped over the white shirt collar sticking out of his black leather jacket.

"I want a girl, just like the girl" started in my head and I shut it off. I could smell peanut butter and toast and coffee on the breath of the kid in the seat behind us who was talking a mile a minute, and there was an odd sound coming from under the floor. Chipped gear in the differential? You notice noises like that when you're on the same bus every morning. The bus picked up speed and the tick, tick, tick, tick accelerated until it blended in with all the other road noises.

HELL'S GATE CANYON

I have a cousin, Arnold, who is considered dangerous. He's over forty now but still lives at home in Morris with his parents who retired there from Swan River when the bank shut down their sawmill. Till he was ten he was a normal kid. No one thought there was anything wrong with him. Except for a slight sensitivity about his face, disfigured in a tractor accident when he was two, no one would have thought twice about him. No more than any one of my father's brothers and sisters do, or their sons. I say sons because the male Regiers tend to be heavy-handed. Roughnecks. The daughters are more delicate, preoccupy themselves with charity projects (Christmas Cheer Boards, the Gospel Mission Centre) and the evangelical charismatic movement. The Regier women can hardly wait to get to church Sunday mornings. They love to call out 'amen' and 'praise God' and clap their hands above their heads in rough time to the preacher's sing-song ecstasy. The men are in on it too. When Swaggart will go down some day because of drugs or women they'll find another TV evangelist to believe in. But it's the men I want to talk about.

Arnold once built a five-storey fort out of eight-foot boards behind his father's sawmill. There was no shortage of materials there. He laid them one on top of the other the way a child builds a house out of popsicle sticks except he didn't glue or nail them because he knew it couldn't be permanent. Each level had a ceiling which then became the floor for the next storey, and each ceiling had a small opening through which to drag up the boards. He was just laying down the ceiling on the fifth floor, twenty-five feet up, intending to go even higher, when the wind blew the whole thing over.

There was a slingshot fight at one of the family gatherings at my house—Regiers versus the neighbourhood. There were eight or nine of us, including Arnold, against as many or more neighbourhood kids. When the Regier cousins came my old friends were enemies. Blood is thicker than water my grandfather always told me and I never doubted it, times like these. A pre-rational primeval kinship force rolled up in us and we were gibbons and orangutans, ancient as gravity as the saying goes. It was dark and we couldn't see much but we fired stones the size of walnuts over and through the lilac hedge that separated our yard and Harold Schellenberg's. After an hour or so of trying to kill each other, an hour interrupted by the odd scream, I suddenly decided I'd had enough when a rock zipped through my hair as I bent to feel for more ammunition.

Arnold was no more crazy than the rest of us though he had more than his share of bad luck growing up. Once he ate most of a bottle of aspirins, unaware of suicide, and had to have his stomach pumped. On another occasion he fell into a cauldron of boiling water that his mother was heating for the laundry. It was one of those big cast-iron pots under which you build a fire and in which you can render the fat from a five-hundred-pound hog. And one Sunday after church when his family was heading for Altwelt to visit us, he fell out of the back door of the car at fifty miles an hour. He was more concerned about his torn new pants than anything when they picked him up.

Once he got into an argument with his brother about his pellet gun. It was powerful enough to shoot right through someone's hand, Arnold said, holding the front of the barrel in his palm. Somehow he pulled the trigger. It didn't quite go through. When he came back from the doctor's, Abe, or Henry, one of his brothers, asked him how he could have been so stupid and while he was explaining that he wasn't stupid, that he'd just been holding the gun against his hand like this and it had gone off, he shot himself again.

But I noticed changes in him as he grew older. Odd things he did and said and peculiar, involuntary motions of his head and hands and feet which he himself wasn't aware of. He became more indignant about insignificant things. What're you staring at, he'd shout suddenly when you happened to be facing in his direction. You hadn't meant to stare. He'd just taken it that way. And in a way his paranoia was reasonable. A network of thin, blue scars etched his forehead. The lines resembled a tangled fishing net.

Abe and Henry had decided to try to start the old tractor that was parked in the vacant lot next door. It was one of those older International Harvesters that still had the two wheels close together in front. Its extra-long rear axle was designed to hold a second set of wheels for wet field work, hauling logs out of the mucky back part of the millyard and that sort of thing. Abe managed to get it started and he chugged around in circles while Henry jogged alongside waiting for his turn. They were both big boys by then, men really. Muscular from helping their father stack cordwood and deliver sawn wood.

Arnold had crawled after them. It was early June with

the grass a foot high or so. When Henry saw Arnold he was only a few feet ahead of the back wheel, laying there hidden in the grass. The front one had missed him. Henry grabbed the extended axle and lifted just as the wheel rolled over Arnold's head.

And Arnold got louder. He comes from a loud family—in fact, the Regiers are all genetically noisy. They're the type that calls across the restaurant to the waitress for water, or talks indignantly about the menu in a Chinese restaurant just when the courteous waiter arrives to take the order. "I don't know if I want anything," he'll say, and then, "They say chicken on the menu but it's probably cat. You can't tell the difference." He'll nod and sweep his eyes around the table expecting the others to be surprised and amazed. Which they often are. Arnold'd talk to you when you were standing right next to him as if you were across the yard. I began to dislike him. He annoyed me and I avoided him.

Arnold is my age, forty-one. When we were sixteen, our two families travelled to British Columbia. A two-car cavalcade. We couldn't really afford to go, my father said, and he made it clear that once we got there we'd have to pick raspberries to pay for the trip. No one complained. We never contradicted my father because in some subtle, unspoken way that was a sin. Besides, the prospect of seeing the mountains for the first time, of seeing an ocean, made any sacrifice trivial, seemed like the very heart of pleasure, pleasure allegorized. It anaesthetized our imaginations. B.C. would be the heaven of fun.

My father had been to the mountains in the mid-thirties when he'd driven his model T across Saskatchewan and Alberta into the foothills near Coleman to stook hay. Ranchers were paying a dollar a day compared to fifty cents in Altwelt, and the difference covered the cost of the gasoline. There's a picture in one of my parents' photo albums, my father's first view of the mountains. They foam up in the distance, barely visible, like a grey water-colour wash. He leans against the side of a dust-coated, narrow-tired black Lizzy, one foot on the running-board, his moustache and smile extravagant as a musketeer's. That was magic to me. That's the smile I always waited to see.

The problem, I felt right away, was that I was going to have to hang around with Arnold. Though I hadn't spent much time with him in the last years, I knew Arnold was sick. They'd taken him out of school the previous year to spend a few months at a mental institution in Winnipeg where we visited him one Saturday. My parents stuck their heads into his room and then left me to entertain him while they headed downtown to shop.

He was lying on a bed in a room which he had to himself. I tried to talk to him but he seemed hard of hearing. There was always a funny pause before he answered me.

"Shocks," he said, when I asked him about the machine in the corner. "I get electric shocks so I'll get better." He showed me the spots on his head where they stuck on the wires and then he twisted and jerked his body to show what happened when they switched the thing on. Scared me into kingdom come. I thought he was having an attack of some sort right in front of me and I was ready to press the button Arnold had shown me that was for calling the nurse. "I hope I don't have to have any more," he said, brushing a hand across his eyes. One of his eyelids fluttered as if it remembered the electricity. "They hurt and they make you dizzy and you can't think for a while," he said. He rolled over on his back facing the ceiling that was white as the bleached strait-jacket that hung beside his bed.

The machine hummed in the corner. I wondered if it hurt more than the time I'd peed against the electric fence in Richard's pasture. Richard lived in Altwelt, too. His family, unlike mine, were farmers. Richard and I had to cross the fence to get to the water-hole to shoot frogs with our slingshots. I pulled up the one chair in the room and sat next to Arnold but I couldn't think of anything to say. A nurse wheeled in a tray of dishes with chrome covers and a glass of purple juice. I didn't want to watch him eat so I said I had to go to the bathroom. I wandered up and down the halls, slow enough so I could get a good look into the open doors at the other sick people, and then sat in one of the waiting rooms reading magazines till my parents came.

Two events during that holiday made me wary of Arnold for the rest of my life. We were in Golden having breakfast. We'd packed up the tents early to get a good start, hoping to get to Abbotsford by dark. There'd been tension between Arnold and his parents while they packed, the sort of anger that, like shaking palsy, you can't quite hide. Arnold swore about the tent he was folding and his father put his arm around his shoulders. Arnold jerked away and told him to F off. I remember thinking that would have been the very last time I would have said that to my father. When the two cars pulled onto the highway Arnold was driving. His father sat in the passenger seat and his mother in the back.

The restaurant was crowded. When the food finally came, my father said grace in a clear voice that I was sure could be heard in the farthest corners of the room. Lord God in Heaven, he prayed, thank you for this opportunity to be with our friends, John and Lena. And Arnold. We're all truly grateful for what you've provided. For this food and for this chance to travel to B.C. together. Help us all to have clean thoughts and a clean mouth. I looked up at Arnold. He was staring at my father. His eyes became slits and his hands, folded out of habit, unfolded and shaped themselves into fists. Arnold hadn't said anything while we waited to be served and he said nothing while we ate. Every few seconds his leg jerked up and he stamped his foot. It was involuntary. He didn't seem to notice that he was doing it. Like a tic of the eye. I wondered how it didn't embarrass him.

It took Arnold two minutes to finish his food. At each mouthful, which he got by lowering his head to his plate so he wouldn't have to raise his fork any more than an inch or two, he peered up at my father. As soon as he'd crammed in the last piece of egg he left the table. He must have weighed two hundred and twenty pounds. His hands, the size of bread-and-butter plates, hung straight down, plumb bobs at the end of long, thick arms. His shoulders sagged as if he were carrying a hundred pounds of flour, he swayed from side to side with each step as if he needed that motion to help him pick up his feet, and his face was bent toward the floor.

Uncle John looked over his shoulder at the door through which Arnold had disappeared. "We had a real bad experience just before we got here," he whispered. He had the round face and puffy wrists of a heavy eater but he'd hardly touched his bacon and eggs. His wife, plump, sad-looking, fifty-five, with grey hair tied back in a tight bun and a hundred wrinkles at the corners of her eyes, laid her hand on his arm.

"John, I don't know if we should bother others with it," she said, concentrating on him, her cheeks turning pink under eyes that seemed to be aware of the door through which Arnold had disappeared. Uncle John didn't look at her. Aunt Lena folded her hands on her lap and looked down at her plate.

"Arnold wanted to drive when we pulled out of the KOA," he said. "I was afraid to let him because of what happened yesterday but I didn't want to get him any more riled than he was already." He picked at an egg with his fork and then pressed down on it to force out the yolk. It cooled and congealed like candle wax as it spread.

"We've had quite a hard time with him lately," he said, and

smiled like people sometimes do the moment after they've heard that a loved one has died. "A really bad time. He's got some mental problems. One day about a month ago he came into our bedroom when I was already at work and Lena was still in bed. He had my .22 and said he was going to shoot her. Thank God Raymond seen him walking past his room. He snuck up behind him and took it away." Aunt Lena put her head in her hands. Her shoulders were shaking.

Uncle John opened his mouth and closed it again, and looked over at his wife. "And now, yesterday, when we went through the Fraser Canyon, before we come to the campground, Arnold was driving." The screen door of the restaurant squeaked. He turned to see who had come in and then faced the table again.

"We got to do what Arnold wants these days. Just when we were by Hell's Gate where there's no guard-rails he suddenly says that now he is going to get even. He'd been waiting for this for a long time and now he is going to drive off the cliff. I said, 'Arnold! Don't say things like that,' and he just laughs and steers the car real close to the edge." Aunt Lena, who'd been whispering to herself while Uncle John talked, wailed. I knew the other tables had noticed.

"I tried to grab the wheel but he pushed me away," my uncle continued, half covering his eyes with one hand. "Then, when I thought for sure this is it, we're going over, he laughs and turns back onto the highway." My uncle laughed too, imitating Arnold's laugh without really meaning to.

Aunt Lena looked at my father and mother, her eyelashes wet. She wasn't aware of me and the other kids. "All I could think of was now we'll soon see Jesus," she said, shaking her head as if disagreeing with herself.

John laid his big red hand on her shoulder. "We been worried sick," he said quietly. "How will we make it through the mountains, Henry?" My father put down his fork. It still had a piece of potato stuck in it and he'd been holding it like that since Arnold had left. He thought for a while with his hands folded as if he were about to pray.

"We're almost through the mountains," he said finally and looked over at us kids. I knew my father. Knew what was coming. This was the man who offered our old neighbour, a woman with stockings that fell around her ankles and who stunk like onions and pigs, a ride to church every Sunday. If we kids objected, which we did every time, he'd say it was our duty as Christians. She was as worthy in God's eyes as any one of us. She'd wait outside by the car till we were ready to go and then squish into the back seat with us. And if she didn't show up on time he'd even drive to her hovel to get her there. For my father the whole world was a mission field.

"Arnold can ride with us," he said. "He won't expect to be able to drive then and he and Peter can keep busy with games or something till we get to Abbotsford." Can't Uncle John control his own kid, I thought. Over the years he'd let him get away with everything and now Arnold was ruling them. I started to object. What person in his right mind would take stuff like this? They probably deserved what they were getting anyway, they'd chosen in the first place to have too many kids. Why always us? But my father interrupted, smiled at my uncle and aunt, and the subject was closed.

When we left the restaurant, Arnold was sitting in the back seat of his parents' car. I decided not to look at him, to pretend he was ordinary, that my life didn't orbit around his. But I couldn't resist. He had a cigarette in his mouth and a *Playboy* magazine on his lap. He must have stolen it, I thought. Doesn't he care if his parents see? It was opened to the picture of a naked woman sitting on a tractor. She was driving away from Arnold and waving with one hand so you could see her bare back and part of one breast. Her face resembled a younger and prettier Aunt Lena.

The other incident that sticks in my head has to do with raspberry picking. We'd been hired by the Latzmans and they'd put up our two families in a couple of empty storage sheds right next to the main house. Our kitchen was a hotplate and a big bowl for washing dishes. Bedrooms were two double bunk-beds that could be separated by hanging a blanket between them. We had to share beds. Roley and I slept on the top of one of the bunks, above Wanda. Thomas, who was the oldest, had the top bunk above my parents.

This was a raspberry-picking trip, my father reminded us kids, including Arnold, on the first morning during breakfast. As much as we'd all like to be free to explore the mountains out there and laze around, each one of us was going to have to pull his weight. We'd get up at 6:00. My father has always liked getting up early and launching right into work without so much as a cup of coffee to loosen him up—always on Saturdays it was, "Got to get up, boys, there's lots to be done. Rise and shine! God loves a willing worker!" We'd be up and we'd pick berries for an hour or two till my mother called us for breakfast, and then get out in the field again all the tedious day long, with an hour break for lunch, till supper at 6:00. Lunch didn't vary much: bologna sandwiches and a family-size can of cold Libby's pork 'n' beans from the case my father had bought when we arrived in Abbotsford. Sometimes as a treat there'd be Watkins orange nectar, one of the products my father sold back home and which he insisted was the best drink in the world. I don't think he'd ever tried any other brands.

We'd finished lunch and were supposed to get back to work in the raspberry patch where the hot, still, blueberry sky and the hot, still air were a bake oven. Where the trees that surrounded the raspberry field—the mountain ash, wild cherry, and Lombardi poplars—walled in heat and walled out even the slightest breeze. Where the sun burned down on your hair like a hot poultice. The dry chicken manure, spread four inches deep between the head-high rows, puffed up at each step and sifted in between your thongs and bare feet. The raspberry prickles, scratching your red arms raw, needled like stinging nettle. The birds stopped singing and the frogs, in the trickle that was left of the creek, quit their croaking by noon. Our parents had already walked the quarter mile to the field. We kids straggled behind, always unwilling to arrive and always pulled there by our mothers' screeches.

Arnold wasn't listening. He headed in the wrong direction when he got out of the bunkhouse and hoisted himself to the top of the Bing cherry tree that took up most of the Latzmans' front yard. There, with a satisfying view of the traffic in the street below, surrounded by black fruit and cool shadows twenty feet up, he lounged like the sultan's favourite son. I followed. He'd done far less than the rest of us in the two weeks we'd been there, fiddling a few berries into a single flat while Wanda and Thomas and Roley and I were forced to fill three, and then loafing in the shaded grass off the field by the fruit-drink jug, smoking without conscience, his mother topping up his half-filled baskets. Or he'd sleep in and after we'd been at it for a couple of hours he'd stroll up, complaining, pick without picking.

"You're supposed to pick too," I yelled. The white sun blazed around the edge of the canopy of leaves. He was hard to see. His shadow blended in with the shadows of the leaves. Something splashed on my forehead. Spit!

"Arnold! I'm gonna get you for that, you asshole," I yelled. "You can't get away with never working and then spit on me." Cherry pits plopped on the grass at my feet. The bugger, I thought, sitting there slurping up cherries. I hate him.

Useless pig. My parents would never let me get away with that. Just because he's a little crazy.

A plum tree grew a few feet away, covered with green fruit the size of small eggs, bigger than any I'd ever seen in Manitoba. I filled my jeans pockets.

"You spit cherries at me," I shouted as I threw a green plum. It sailed past him, swished through the leaves, an arrow from Robin Hood's bow, and landed in the street below.

"We're all supposed to help and you too," I yelled, and threw another.

It connected and he roared. "Get lost, you prick, I'm not coming down." A handful of uneaten cherries rained down on me. "Get away from me, you suck." He was egging me on. Daring me to throw again. This one missed.

"When I catch you, you're gonna pay," he yelled, shaking his fist down at me and making threatening movements as if he were about to climb down. There was a happiness in his voice that made me shiver. He could hardly wait to get his hands on me. I knew I should run but I couldn't. There were a few plums left in my pocket and first I had to use them up. When I threw again the plum winked up toward Arnold's shadow and this time the thud was solid. There was silence. A blackbird chuck, chuck, chucked. My mother screamed at me from far away in the field. A white Collins' Berry Farm truck whizzed by on the road.

"Arnold," I called. No answer. At the moment that I turned to go I saw his shadow sway, twist, arms down and loose, and separate itself from the branch he'd been sitting on. It looped downward. Toward me. Leaves rustled, branches shook and cracked, and then in a rush it took on colour, somersaulting like a falling doll. I was already stepping toward him as he thunked to the ground. He lay still, his eyes wide and green and steady. I turned and ran to the shed where we slept. There were empty Libby's pork 'n' beans cans, dirty paper plates and unwashed forks on the plywood sheet. My mother had been in too much of a hurry to wash the dishes. She'd apologize to my father when they came in from the patch. I crawled in under my parents' bunk. From far away came the murmur of the women talking to each other while they picked berries in the heat.

THE OCTOBER REBELLION

The Morden Civic Centre did double duty as a post office and a court-house, suggesting even in this the pervading hypocrisy that bothered me then about small-town Manitoba and bothers me now. Outside, it was all brick and stone, all cornices and gargoyles and high stairs, all deep-set windows and brass door fittings. But the inside was rococo and worn. There was fir trim, its varnish almost worn off, once-white buffalo-board ceiling tiles, and creaky floorboards that looked black through doorways. Left of Judge Thompson's desk stood an imitation brick fireplace with cast-iron logs that darkened and brightened in the blue-orange light of the rotating foil. On the panelling behind the judge's head flickered the memory of a smoky gaslight. And then the finishing touch. Under the high ceiling, their torsos ghost-like, their eyes shining, hung old portraits, in heavy plaster frames, of past notaries. Jurors at my trial.

Judge Thompson ignored us at first and then studied me for a while before he spoke, as he might criticize slabs of beef

hanging in a butcher shop he wouldn't ordinarily consider
going into. "We already know everything from the others," he
grunted, raising a lazy, tobacco-stained finger till it pointed
at my chest. "We're just checking your story. Why don't you
first tell us what happened?" He paused, out of breath after
each sentence, and dug in the irritated crevices of his
Hitchcock double chins with a handkerchief clamped in a fat
hand. Drops of sweat glistened like maggots on his forehead
and clung to the red welts of wrinkles there. His breath stank.
Even ten feet away it withered good intention and dizzied
concentration. He must have rooted in a manure pile for his
lunch, I thought as I waited there. I wondered if there were
tell-tale signs on the knees of his seersucker.

The gang of Altwelt kids that I hung around with and a
few strays that we picked up along the way had decided to
"give 'er" on what we figured might well be our last
Hallowe'en night together. The group was made up of town
kids and village kids. Town and village. That was a distinction
that had seemed important when we were younger but had
blurred and disappeared over the years. There was Pancho,
whose mother complained about how short her neighbour's
daughters wore their skirts and who hiked her own up way
above her knees out of thoughtfulness to us boys, and who
once took a potshot at the girls with Pancho's .22. There was
Yardstick, the only kid I knew whose parents were separated,
and whose nickname would make an interesting story in
itself. And Trotter, whose father had been the Co-op gas truck
driver till he'd retired a few years before.

We were all around sixteen, tough. It was nothing for me
to run the two miles to town and back for cigarettes. Sap
siphoned up out of the pagan Hallowe'en ground through the
holes in our Eaton's Supertreads as if it were spring. We each
supplied something: water-filled balloons, a bull-horn, a
bucket of sloppy pig manure, and so on. Richard Stoez, who

lived at the end of the village farthest away from town, supplied the truck. A yellow '59 Ford half-ton with a souped-up '55 Chevy 283. It had oversized pistons and a racing cam and it had left Sergeant Esawchuk coughing like an asthmatic in the dust more than once.

Judge Thompson waited. The finger covering me dropped slowly under the weight of his arm. "Well, we set off a few firecrackers in Altwelt and then drove around the country for a while," I said, pretending to be convinced, a cold shiver between my shoulder-blades. The portraits above me seemed to shift from place to place in the blurry spaces around the edge of my glasses.

"Where did you throw them?" he asked. A sick yellow light made a sort of halo on the oak desk.

"Close to the school, I think." I squinted as if trying to remember and pushed my glasses higher up on my sweaty nose with a middle finger. The significance of that struck me only after I'd done it and was happily lost on the judge.

"Wasn't it closer to the Bergthaler Church?" The judge's eyes were the same yellow as the light on his desk.

I looked at the floor. "I guess so," I said finally.

"In fact, it was in the Bergthaler Church! Right?" I avoided his eyes and glanced up at the dim shadows under the ceiling. It's all over, I thought.

Nobody ever had two cents to rub together so we stole the firecrackers. The only place in town that sold them was Jacobs's Pub, which wasn't a pub at all but a miniature general store. Jacobs must have survived on his sale of firecrackers because nobody ever seemed to buy anything else there. In 1963 the Jam-Jams, Chocolate Puffs, Cream Delights and Red Sugar Cookies in the six glass jars underneath the National Cash Register looked like the same ones I'd seen there in 1955. They had the same sick, grey pallor as

Jacobs's skin. Richard pretended his parents wanted him to try on a new pair of canoe boots and while Jacobs shuffled to the back with him I pocketed a handful of Hong Kong Flamers and Inch-longs.

On the way to the Mayflower Inn to pick up the others, we detoured past the church to look in on the Bergthaler Young People's Hallowe'en Social. To see how the suckers were doing who had to spend this most exquisite evening of the year indoors playing board games, bobbing for apples, and hunting black and orange jellybean-trail treasure. On impulse, either out of an evangelical urge to liven up the evening for the shut-ins or a sadistic need to let them know what they were missing, we lit a package of chain crackers, a hundred inch-longs on a continuous fuse, and pitched them into the vestibule. The rat-a-tat explosions faded behind us as we fled toward the truck parked a block away in the alley behind Trotter's back yard.

"And then we picked up a few other kids at the Mayflower and drove to Gretna," I said, hoping he'd let it go at that. The cleaning ladies had tried to get the lamp burns off the wall a hundred times, judging from the scratches and dullness of the spot above his head, I thought. My feet felt tired in my old black and white runners, no arch supports, and I had a hard time deciding what to say.

"Just a minute," the judge interrupted. He patiently stroked a small section of the desk top with one hand as if it were a kitten and he held the other under his nose, sniffing its nicotine stain. "Don't you know how dangerous that could have been?" He took a slow, deep breath. "It's just lucky you didn't burn the whole building to the ground, kids and all!" He paused again, waiting for an answer. His eyes filed away at mine, and his finger aimed at a spot between them. I couldn't decide which foot to balance on. "Is that what you wanted?" he barked when I didn't speak. My father's arched eyebrows echoed the question.

"No, we didn't want to burn anything. We just did it, that's all," I said. My voice was too high and I couldn't keep the words from tumbling over each other. My chest felt tight and small. The watch I'd gotten for Christmas out of the Regal catalogue suddenly ticked loudly. I noticed that my father's shoes didn't need polishing. He always kept them shiny.

The judge slumped back and shook his head, eyes closed, shutting out the room, the world. Like teachers and preachers, judges are good actors. They wag yellowing moral fingers at slight crimes but you know they really are deciding to get more sleep this night than last or debating whether a bit of extra star anise might make the borscht taste the way it used to. His fingertips touched under his chins as if in prayer, bracing the weight of his head and neck.

"Well, go on," he sighed, looking down at his pillow of a paunch and giving his grey vest a tug.

There were thirteen of us in the truck, four in the cab and nine on the box, otherwise we wouldn't have tackled old Groening's cultivator. We took the seven miles of back roads into the neighbouring town of Gretna instead of the 14A. The night was moonlit black and Indian summer warm. We were travelling fast. I stood with my head and shoulders above the cab and the wind pushed against my face and made my hair go the way Peter Fonda's does in *Easy Rider*. Gravel drummed underneath the floor. The barking of a dog filled and emptied the night in the seconds we took to pass its farm. It was Hallowe'en and we felt no fear, nothing wrong. This was no *Fall of the House of Usher* for us. If Roderick's friend had crossed that singularly dreary tract of country with a train of knights like ours, he wouldn't have given lurid tarns and ghastly grey sedges a second glance. Strength in numbers, as the saying goes.

I was picturing that witch, Mary Jane Martins, in a loose-fitting ghost's sheet when we surged forward against the cab. The truck lurched sideways and settled like the end of an elevator ride.

"There's no lights at Gus's and he's got no dog," Richard called, not too loud, his head stuck through the open side window. Some of the guys had already jumped off before the truck came to a stop and others were still standing on the box, not sure whether to get off. Trotter stepped to the grassy edge of the road to urinate.

"Trotter's got no pressure," Pancho said, giggling, poking at his seat with his thumb. "Hey, guys, come have a look!" Trotter stood there for a while and then pulled it back in without finishing.

We crossed some barbed wire and a stretch of pasture in the dark on our way to Gus's yard, ducking low and running with bent knees, and then crowded up against what the sharp smell and sudden gruntings inside told us was the back of the pig barn.

"We've got enough to tip this thing," someone said. Silence. This was bigger than we'd imagined. But we grabbed hold where we could on the tiny flanges of rotting shiplap and rocked the building till it tilted into its own front yard. Into the mud the pigs had made. Half a dozen yearlings zipped out from underneath, squealing, bunched like porpoises. Their lipless, sickle mouths, half open, scythed toward the far corner of the pit. There the pigs froze, huddled, staring back at their tumbled house. They seemed intent and curious as if wondering how quickly renovations take place in the world. Two weeks from now they would be under the farmer's knife and on the neighbours' tables.

At the main barn, the overhang gave us the most trouble.

The first eight feet were all right because the cultivator wheels actually rode up the wall, but then the hitch and tines caught under the eaves.

"Turn it upside down, guys. That way maybe we can get the points to hang onto the roof," Richard said. He had a practical mind, predictable as old man Friesen who lived with his two sisters half-way down the village road. Why none of them ever married we could only guess. You never saw them out of doors before noon or after supper-time, and there was never a light on inside their faded yellow house. Never. They went to bed when it got dark. Their old whale-shaped grey Pontiac headed downtown to the post office every afternoon at 3:00, putzing along at a pace that didn't raise the dust, twenty years of whining along in first gear.

Richard was a born supervisor. He never worked, pushing this or lugging that, those things were for others. He stood on the sidelines making improvements.

The toughest guys—and I don't think any of us weighed two hundred pounds, not a hockey player in the bunch—stood underneath and pushed up. The rest worked from the top with the ropes we'd found in the lean-to. We strained and swore and finally one tine hooked over the tin rain trough, and then another, and then enough so that the centre of balance tipped the whole thing level. We jockeyed the cultivator further up the slope, using the wheels now, and then there it was. All thirteen of us stood on the roof and admired our handiwork.

"Shit, nobody's ever put something this big on a roof on Hallowe'en before," Richard said. "Nobody. This is the biggest. What'll old Gus think tomorrow, eh?" Then we raced for the safety of the road.

"You did what?" the judge roared. His fists on the desk, clenched as if they were holding a fork and knife, pounded out the rhythm of the words.

"We burned some bales," I said, looking at the jury above his head.

"So! That was your group! Ooooo! That's bad! Did you think of the motorists? Eh? The motorists?" He liked the taste of 'motorists' and he smacked his lips every time he said it. "And what if the whole pile had started? Heh?" He bent forward slowly, his paunch slipping under the desk, and tried to touch my chest with his finger. "What would Mr. Janzen do if his barn had burned? Did you think of that?" He sank back into his high black chair, puffing.

"Well," I said, trying to smooth things over, wondering what the fine would be, "it was just some straw bales on the road. We didn't think anyone would mind a few straw bales." What was so damned dangerous, anyway, I thought. Not nearly as bad as the grain auger we'd rolled across the mile road at Gnadenthal. It blended into the night, invisible until you were right on it. That one had worried me. No one would hit a pile of blazing straw that you could see for five miles. Lucky for me, Judge Thompson's information stopped short of the auger.

We were already back at the truck when we saw lights down the road. Till then we hadn't considered the danger, hadn't thought how hard it is to see a dirty, red machine after dark. Three of us raced back. The lights were close. Too close.

"We're not going to make it," Trotter squealed, and we knew he was right. So we just stood and waited, not together, but where each of us had stopped. Waited for the impact. For the auger to jump through the air and for the car to skid, slough through the ditch, and turn tires over roof into the pasture. Like a canoe caught in bushes at the lip of the falls, we waited for the inevitable. We were as certain of renovation as the pigs had been. But, at the last second the car braked, swerved once left, and picked up speed again toward Altwelt. We rolled the auger off the road.

"Regier, come give us a hand," Trotter called from the darkness of the field. I was sitting in the ditch beside the truck which stood by the edge of the highway, too clearly in view for my liking. Already, two miles south at Gretna, headlights curved onto the pavement and headed in our direction. We had two minutes at most. There were ten or so guys running with bales and the pile was two wide and three high. I jogged down the bank to join them, scared of something. Scared suddenly we'd be caught. The cultivator had been all right and so had the firecrackers because there we'd been invisible. Gus hadn't been home and he had no nearby neighbours. And at the church it was simply heave them in and split. But this was too dangerous a rebellion.

You could see both headlights now. Half a mile of time. The pile was five rows high. We crouched down on the lee side with matches and the dry straw swirled into quick flame. Richard had the truck revving and he roared away while we were still clambering up. Through the back window I saw the speedometer. The red surged laterally up past the ranks of green irradiant numbers, eighty, ninety, a hundred, and disappeared to the right of a hundred and twenty. If we were to flip now, would I survive? How could you know without trying it? Tuck your knees against your chest, wrap your arms around them and roll through the knee-high yellow hay grass of the road allowance like a rubber tire? Slaloming around hydro poles and moguling over approaches, ending up tipped over on your side, laughing, in a black-plowed field?

The judge called me a public nuisance, said I was lucky getting off lightly, and fined me ten dollars. On the way to the car I promised myself I'd be careful not to get into trouble anymore, and I promised my father to repay the loan from my beet-weeding money. After that we walked in silence and I watched his glossy shoes step carefully around wetter spots where the snow had melted. My father's station wagon was parked near the Morden Mennonite Brethren Church. As I opened the door to get in, I saw Pastor Braun on the church steps talking to Molly Thompson, the judge's daughter. A sudden gust of wind lifted her blue shift above her slender knees and she dropped an ineffectual hand to hold it down. The see-through orange scarf that had covered her blonde hair fluttered to her feet and tangled itself in the wrought-iron handrail. Pastor Braun smiled up at her as he bent down.

CRAZY CREEK

Most of you know the creek or at least have seen it though you probably don't remember the name. It's one of those little glacial rivers that comes tearing down off the mountains somewhere between Revelstoke and Golden. That's mad country in there. The mountains loom and glower and the creeks deceive. They look so much less dangerous from the road than when you actually leave the car and, made cocky somehow by the pastoral sun, green jingle of spruce, and the wide clearances they build at these "natural beauty spots" to trap the tourist into stopping and taking pictures—they must think all travellers are Japanese or from the prairies—you want to wade into them. What looks a foot or two deep because it's the clearest ice water is really five or six feet of current.

They lure, but you don't want to step in them any more than Verna and I actually wanted to hike to the bottom of the Grand Canyon on our honeymoon. A six-mile trek down and a nine-mile one up by an alternate route. A hundred and five in the shade. Canteen empty before you're half-way back. We would never have been tempted to do it if it hadn't been for those pay binoculars at the top which draw the Colorado River in so close and peaceful.

My ten-year-old son almost drowned in a creek like that near Hope a few years ago. We'd come all the way from Kelowna that day and it was blistering so we stopped at a wayside picnic site and waded into this creek. The current pulled harder than I'd expected and the round boulders under my feet rolled when I touched them. I was turning to get out when I heard Jamie yell. There he was, just beyond reach, hanging onto a rock, only his head above water. One minute he was somewhere safe on my right, the next he'd been sucked past me and was almost gone, clutching this submerged rock.

After my experience at the creek I started out telling you about, when I was nineteen or so, I thought I'd never forget anything about that place. I memorized all its landmarks as we were leaving. But to tell you the truth, I can't remember where it is. It's somewhere between those two towns, that's all I know.

My parents live in Chilliwack now in semi-retirement and I and my wife and kids have often driven the Roger's Pass. Every time we do I suddenly remember and decide to point it out to the others. To tell them, see, that's where it happened. And every time, because all the spots begin to look the same after a while, I start wondering if I've missed it. Did you see the sign yet, I'll ask Verna. Were you watching the road the whole time? I didn't think it was this far.

What I do recall is that before you get to it you come to an overpass made of logs. Not a traffic intersection, but one of those bridges that must have been used at one time by logging trucks or maybe it was part of the old Trans-Canada. It's weathered and ragged and inviting like so much in the B.C. mountains, but even then, twenty years ago, you wouldn't have dared drive across it. About a mile further you come to a concrete bridge, set quite high up over a gorge, with one of those green signs that says CRAZY CREEK.

It was almost dark. Every time we rounded an outside curve the green and purple sky, in the last stages of twilight, swayed into view ahead like gambling booths seen from a merry-go-round. At the inside curves the sky hid itself again behind the black hulk of the mountain. The radio reception had been shaky since Banff, even on my Blaupunct, but now towards evening it was clearing. The announcer from the Revelstoke station was playing some great driving music. Derek and the Dominoes. "Key to the Highway." I love the way that song opens. After the electric bottleneck guitar plays its five minutes of walking blues and almost convinces you that this is an instrumental, Clapton's voice, reminiscent of Dylan, slips in slow and sad:

> I got the key to the highway
> I'm billed out and bound to go
> I'm gonna leave here runnin'
> Cause walkin' is most too slow

The music, nobody on the road, heading for Tofino, a hundred sweet dangers to survive. Clapton might be thinking about leaving the group because his musical interests are changing direction, the announcer was saying. Everything felt great. Peaceful. Under control. I wasn't exactly sleepy, just relaxed. Really relaxed. Should I stop and open a Club? There wouldn't be any cops around at this time of the night. I was still thinking about it when the steering-wheel jerked left and almost wrenched itself out of my hands. The car veered toward the cliff, unresponsive and lopsided as a tug-boat. Bodies, luggage, loose things flung themselves from side to side as I wrestled with the wheel. Jacob and his angel. The headlights shone alternately on rock wall and trees and into black space. Finally, the car slowed, straightened out, and it was over. I rolled the Volkswagen as close as I could to the mountain. No one in the car was hurt and after we'd agreed that we'd had a blowout we were all silent. We just sat there looking out the car windows, none of us facing the mountain.

I'd thought about the bald tires before we left but had expected we'd make it somehow. I was cocky, you know, the way kids are. If we didn't make it there and back, we all had to die sometime. That wasn't good or bad, just how it was. But now events jerked around frighteningly. Things, death, come on you unexpectedly, I thought. This one could have gone either way. The valley at dusk had been indistinct, less ominous in the dark than by daylight, but we'd come close enough to the edge for me to see the lights of the town way ahead and very straight down. "Key to the Highway" was still soughing out one of its eight verses. I shut the radio off and opened my window. The high-altitude air cooled my nose and throat and the night, empty of even the sound of birds or frogs or beetles, empty as the Bergthaler church during the week, seemed too dark and quiet.

Teenagers don't think, really. Aren't perspicacious or fore-sightful. Don't find things daunting. That Volkswagen bug was ten years old. The part that still had some colour was a sun-faded blue. The piston pressure hovered somewhere around eighty in the cylinders. The handbrake didn't work. The suspension was shot and at level crossings, even carrying only the driver, the rear end slammed down on the frame so hard you could chip your teeth. The front part of the curved hood and the bottom edge at the back where the fenders are bolted to the rest of the body were brittle with rust.

For this trip we'd overloaded it, crammed it from top to bottom, and so it was top-heavy, almost uncontrollable. Worse than Tom Joad's jalopy in *The Grapes of Wrath*. Besides the four of us, we'd squeezed in a heavy four-man canvas tent (my family had used it since I was a kid and it wasn't rainproof anymore), tent poles, campstove, Coleman lantern, sleeping bags, fishing rods, tackle boxes, pillows, suitcases, bags with odds and ends like sunflower seeds, chocolate bars and fruit, a twenty-four of beer, and on and on. At the last minute we'd decided against the canoe because we needed the roof for gear. The trunk up front wouldn't close and had to be tied down. Whichever two happened to be in the back seat had to sit on sleeping bags with their heads butted against the roof and their necks bent.

We didn't have enough gas money among us to make it back. But the wild, incredible ocean, thousands of un-restrained, uninterrupted miles of it between Japan and Vancouver Island breaking on Long Beach, unpeopled Long Beach, was as irresistible as secret love. Nanaimo, Campbell River, Eureka, all those magic places to see. What was money? We'd collect mussels and oysters when we got to the ocean, steal a chicken in Salmon Arm, lift a few cans of pork 'n' beans at a Safeway in Regina if we had to. Hell, we could spend half a day collecting beer bottles along the Trans-Canada at Moose Jaw. A case of empties would get you a gallon of gas and a gallon of gas would take you thirty, thirty-five miles easy. We'd make it.

Only I don't believe it, not now. Volkswagens are death-traps. Each time I've owned one it's almost killed me. But I continued to buy them for years. Stupid. I successively owned five bugs before I finally broke the habit and bought a Dodge Valiant.

The month I turned sixteen my older brother, Thomas, took Roley and me fishing in the Whiteshell in his lime green bug. We couldn't believe our luck. Thomas was an over-achiever and much too busy ever to have fun, I thought. Now again, as always, he had one bit of irrelevant business after another to finish before we could get going. We'd only driven about thirty miles when he asked me to take over so he could sleep. And then I more or less wrecked the car.

You know that dead-end junction a mile north of Beausejour? By the time we got to it I was basically asleep too, mesmerized by the white dotted line and intent on keeping the car to the right of it. I looked up in time to see the stop sign sleepwalk by, hit the brakes and holy shit, we flew into space. A telephone pole floated through the head-lights and passed by my side window. A thud, a splash, water, mud, bulrushes whipping over the windshield. We'd dropped ten feet, hit the ditch that runs on straight ahead of where our road ended, and surfed along a hundred yards. The twenty-four of Cokes, mostly broken, the luggage and the three of us were piled in the front seat. The back seat was empty. Water seeped in through the door.

Something like this, I guess. The mountain air was damned cold and the sleeping bags we'd taken with us—mine came from a Woolco sale—were definitely not meant for this. We lay there on the stony edge of the road trying to keep warm, trying to sleep. What a lousy trip. How could we have thought it'd be fun? Stuck two miles up with a car that probably wouldn't get us home and no money to fix it. We'd decided not to bother trying to get anyone to stop. They wouldn't even look at us in the dark and, anyway, no service station'd be open to fix the spare. The night dragged on. The odd car or semi wailed by. No one said much. Benny suggested building a fire for something to do and to get us warmed up. No one answered. We huddled in our bags, drinking beer till it got too cold to even want to do that.

Towards morning, when light was just beginning to show us the trees and the borders of the mountains and the road, a car passed and then braked and backed to where we had ours jacked up.

I was the oldest so it was up to me to take the ride. I hated hitch-hiking. Hated meeting strangers, paranoid, especially off the prairie, of weirdos. In the light that came on when the car door opened I checked over the driver. The man inside was about sixty, wearing a suit jacket and tie and a narrow-brimmed fake fur hat. The kind my father wore. They were always popular among upwardly mobile Mennonite men who had somehow escaped the farm and ventured into small business. He smiled and asked with real concern what our trouble was. Sure, he'd give me and my tire a ride into Revelstoke. It's only ten, fifteen miles, he said. This'd be all right, I thought. It wasn't a young woman but it wasn't a bum or a carload of bums either. I slid the tire through the back seat door and we left with the other three guys standing beside the road, yelling at me to hurry back.

I've always sensed that B.C. is a haven for the depraved. Full of Charles Mansons, Clifford Olsens and Reverend Jameses. No daily takes as much pleasure as the *Vancouver Sun* in its accounts of axe murders, widow assaults, child molestings, violent rapes, and murder rituals they call religion. Look at the premiers—wacky Bennett, Vander Zalm—they don't come any loonier. It seems as though homicidal types sail into port every day by the boat-load, generate like babies in the hash-smoking communes north of Hazelton, natural by-products of the dock workers' unions and the logging industry. The very land, postcard pretty, dreamland for pre-TV, for southern Manitoba farmboys, is rotten to the core.

You cannot love God and Mammon both, my mother liked to say (the Bible always seemed to open to that one for her) and this national corruption seems to be the tailings of primary industry itself—a product of the gold and copper barely hidden, Saskatchewan topsoil deep, inside every mountain, the car-thick trees or stumps of trees that make up the coastal forests, the tens of thousands of miles of salmon-coagulated rivers that churn through the gorges of Lillouet, Chilcotin and Skeena. It's all there. All the evils of West Coast idleness.

I had reason to feel sick now too. Before we'd gone a hundred yards, the driver felt between his legs. Scratching himself, I thought, but worried right away that he was a pervert. And then he pulled out a beer bottle. Even with that little distraction the car began to wander. It was half-way over the dotted line before he noticed and straightened it out. It didn't take long to realize he had no control over the car. He'd make a correction and then it would sidle even farther into the passing lane. Once we were so far over that the tires kicked up gravel from the wrong shoulder. I imagined stones dropping thousands of feet to the dark valley floor. This was exactly what I'd been afraid of all my life. This was it.

During the worst of it, we were in the passing lane and approaching an outside curve. The speedometer showed sixty. Surely he'd move over, see the danger, have enough instinct to pull back. But he didn't seem to notice a thing. I forgot courtesy and yelled. At the last second, at the very last possible moment in which something could have been done, he jabbed his beer bottle between his legs and lolled the wheel. The tires churned in the gravel next to the cliff edge and the car sulked back into its proper lane. To him, unruffled, oblivious of death, this was old hat. "Let me off," I shouted, and then, only then, he reacted with energy.

"I saw your frickin Manitoba licence plate," he roared. "You're all chickenshits. What the hell's the matter with you? *You* lecturing *me* on drinking? I'm a better driver for chrissake when I've had a drink or two. You wanted a ride, right?" he yelled. "You want to walk all the way into town?" He looked straight at me as if I had committed some unspeakable act, ignoring the road. The bottle was empty when he lifted it to his mouth and he opened a window and chucked it over the cliff. I didn't answer him, just sat there bent forward, staring straight ahead. Morning light glared purple along a crack in the windshield.

He changed his tone, almost whining. "Hey, don't worry," he said, "I'll get you there safe. Honest. Look, I never even had an accident in my life but if you're scared I'll slow down. Promise."

And he did. Thirty still seemed hellish fast to me but it took the edge off my worry. When we finally pulled into the Texaco station on the main street I jumped out before the car stopped rolling. I felt justified but guilty. Like a little girl trying to convince someone that the man pulling at her arm really isn't her father. It wasn't easy, he was persuasive, but I turned down his offer to drive me back to my car once they'd finished patching the spare.

After we got the tire back on and were driving down off the mountain we decided to splurge on a restaurant breakfast this once. By the time the waitress brought coffee and took our orders some of the mystery that had urged us to leave Altwelt in the first place was beginning to seep back in. The morning sun lit up the tops of the close mountains, and gas bowsers threw long shadows across the ditch and up onto the highway. A few blackbirds pecked at the gravel beside the pumps. It was still early and there was no traffic to speak of. We were almost the only travellers up at this time of day, I thought. We had more will-power than most people, that was it. They'd start pulling in for breakfast about the time we were finishing and we'd have been making headway for an hour before they even hit the road, the bums.

The waitress came with the bacon and eggs. Her red lipstick

and red nail polish were nice but seemed out of place this early. She was half-way back to the counter when I called her and asked for four glasses of water. She sighed, but nodded.

"Let's stop at one of those creeks and do some exploring," I said. Gary and Roley nodded, kept eating. Roley was inter-ested in the waitress. She was serving a trucker who had just pulled in. He'd parked his rig in front of the window where it blocked the view of the mountains. It was an Allied Van Lines truck and all you could see was the orange side of the trailer with a black highway and white dotted lines disappearing from sight painted on it. Benny didn't agree right away. He took off his glasses and wiped them on a serviette and then slipped them back on, using both hands as if he were scared the glasses would break. The gold wire arms were bent and frail-looking.

"I don't know," he faltered. "Don't we want to get to the coast as soon as we can?" He dipped down low over his plate, almost cringing, to take a bite of the sandwich he'd made with his sunnyside-up egg and toast, and peeked at me out of the tops of his eyes. A bit of bright yolk trickled from a corner of his mouth. His eyes wavered when he looked at anything for more than a moment. He reminded me of my boyhood neighbour's, Harold's, dog. It had been kicked so often that it would only creep. It would slither by the whole front of our yard along the gravel road. I'd checked once, and its belly fur was all rubbed off.

"Benny, we've got all the time in the world," I said, laugh-ing. "You're on vacation now. Take it easy, enjoy yourself. This isn't like working, you know."

Benny didn't find it funny and just bent further over his egg and bread. Roley smiled but managed to keep from putting in his two cents' worth.

"Hey, Benny, you've got your whole life ahead of you, you want to jump from one job to the next?" I winked over Benny's bent head at the others. The waitress giggled at something the trucker said and her red fingers flashed to her red mouth. Benny peeked with a wide unfocussed eye in her direction but he wasn't looking quite in the right place. She headed back toward the counter, straightening chairs as she went.

Benny had been a last-minute addition. Knowing what I did about him, I wondered why Roley and Gary had even thought of him. He didn't really fit in. But it wasn't my decision. I was the older brother in this case, Roley's older brother, and didn't have much to do with the kids. Because I was heading west anyway, I'd thought, why not offer them an opportunity they'd really appreciate. And anyway, I could use the extra cash and drivers. But Benny?

Though Benny was older than me he hung around with the sixteen-year-olds. He was quiet, gentle, said nothing until he was sure that you could be trusted not to tease him and then his words fell over each other the way his feet did. Somehow he'd never learned to walk with ease. The cowboy boots he wore everywhere from the day he got a job as camp wrangler looked too heavy for him. He lifted his feet half a second later than common grace demanded and set them down the same length of time too late. His eyes bulged behind his glasses, stared out oversized and timid and watery.

Benny worked summers at the Barwaldy Bible Camp. He'd been put in charge of the horses and archery and campfires and he loved it. Revelled in his sudden authority. Bathed in the adulation of the young campers. They loved him too because he related to them as if kids really mattered. Not quite as though they were his age, but as if he knew exactly how they felt inside. He seemed like a child who'd been given responsibilities and he was good at his job. No one could have taken more pride in any work than Benny did. He deserved more than he got.

So this summer was a change for him. He was taking his

first vacation from Barwaldy and his first trip with a bunch of guys. He and his mother were both excited. "Benny's never gone anywhere with friends before," she told me in private when we stopped at his house to pick him up. "He's so pleased! God bless you for taking him along, Peter!" I wanted to get going but stood quietly listening to her and felt proud I'd considered her enough to do that.

"Be careful, though," she said as I got into the too-small bucket seat behind the wheel, and I nodded. "He's not supposed to exert himself too much because of his condition, okay?"

After passing by a number of streams, passing by them almost before we saw them, before we could decide, we chose Crazy Creek. The ditch was pretty with its close-cut grass and daisies sprinkled thicker under the bridge where there was more shade and out along the border of the forest. The birds sang the way they do on calm, warm mornings, so clear and brilliant you're tempted to cover your ears. The pines and spruce sprayed perfume like musk, seduced you into their mossiness, the ancient bower of bliss, the B.C. Highways Department's *hortus conclusis*. The river, hidden by a tumble of boulders a few hundred yards uphill, sloped from the mountain, quiet and wild at the same time. The grade seemed oddly steep and shallow.

At first we just played at the edge of the water. Dug in the sand for wet, coloured stones, paddled with bare feet in the pools at the creek edge, stuck our dusty heads into water that swirled cold as if it had come out of a refrigerator. But this laziness didn't satisfy us for long.

"Let's go higher up," Roley said. "See where this thing comes from. It looks like easy climbing." Benny looked at me to see if I agreed. He turned toward Gary. Turned his whole body so he was facing him. He was thinking hard about something and his eyes began to waver. He made a decision of some sort without speaking and started back toward the car. He was careful to step around the clumps of daisies in his path.

Roley was already up where the creek bent out of sight. He came to a fallen tree that blocked his way and sat down on it to get over easier. He swung his legs up, looked back and saw that Benny was walking the wrong way.

"Hey, Benny, aren't you coming?" he called. "Come on, come on, let's all go." Benny kept on walking, though he turned his head to look. "Benny, look, we'll go slow if you're worried about staying behind. Honest. No problem. Come on, you can do it. It won't be that hard. Come on." Benny stopped. He wasn't sure. He took off his glasses and wiped them on his shirt.

"Come awwwnn," Roley called again, his voice falling in such a way you wouldn't want people to see you ignoring what he said. This time Benny turned around.

For a while we followed a footpath. When it petered out we had to pick our way now along the edge of the creek, now higher up. At first we talked and laughed but after an hour or so we were out of breath and a bit spooked and the talking stopped. A few times Benny called to us to slow down. We did, but then forgot and picked up our pace again. When we were almost at the top, I looked back. Benny was fifty yards behind me, sitting on the grass beside the path.

"Hey, you tired?" I called. "We can wait if you want. Take a rest. Then we'll go on." I was winded myself and breathing hard and the words came out in spurts. Benny didn't answer and I walked back towards him. Sunlight brightened his legs, the rest of him sat in the shadow of some pines. Even after the hike his blue jeans looked neat and pressed. Some people have a way of staying tidy. His carrot-coloured hair was matted with sweat and his face seemed as red as his hair. Despite the heat, he had his sleeves rolled down and buttoned at his wrists and throat. Further down the path a raven lifted from a low branch and sailed, without cawing, in the direction we'd come from.

"You go on," he whispered, his voice husky, tired. "I'll stay here. I'll be okay again when you get back." He sighed and lay back in the grass. He pulled his straw cowboy hat over his face.

I waited a moment and then followed Gary and Roley who hadn't noticed that we weren't with them. What's the matter with that guy, anyway, I thought. He's this far, may as well go to the top. Sure he's tired, but he just needs a little rest. Nobody's in that much of a hurry that we couldn't wait a bit. I mean, it's vacation time, we don't have to push ourselves. You'd think he'd want to tell his mom that he'd climbed to the top of a mountain. Some people think funny.

The view was spectacular at the top. The creek roared along a straight stretch out almost as far as we could see and then disappeared behind another mountain a mile or so in the distance. On the horizon, a dozen other peaks reared up. The valley, green and black with spruce, was an endless forest that stretched north all the way to Prince Rupert and beyond. What a wild place this B.C. was. When I wasn't here, when I was on the prairies, I wanted to live here. Now, though, this was plenty. I didn't need it as my back yard. This was good enough. We'd done what we set out to do.

Suddenly, I was bored. Wanted to get back down to the car. Hit the road.

"Hey, I wonder what the girls are up to on Long Beach," I said as I turned and ran down the easy path that made up that highest stretch of the mountain. The others followed, raced to catch me, unwilling to be the last one on the mountain. We ran till we got to Benny.

"Wake up," Roley yelled as he passed. "Time to get moving." But then he turned and came back to where Gary and I were standing. Benny stared up at us with steady eyes as blue as the Okanagan Lake on a sunny day. They didn't waver and he didn't move.

Gary nudged him with his foot. "Benny, hey come on, aren't you rested yet?"

I knelt down to get a closer look at his eyes and mouth. They were too still, too fixed.

"Something's happened. Something's wrong." On the back of my neck it felt cool as if a winter breeze had just begun to blow. I bent and put my ear on his chest. Nothing. I touched his wrist. Nothing.

"He's dead," I said, looking up at Gary and Roley who stood beside Benny, quiet as trees.

"What will we tell his mom?" Gary said. He stood looking down at Benny, not touching him, not bending to check if I might be wrong.

"This is bad," Roley said. "What happened? He must have had a heart attack. He once had rheumatic fever. He shouldn't have climbed so high." He knelt and put his hand inside Benny's shirt over his heart. "What are we going to do now?" he asked. He got up and stood there, half facing the car. "Does this mean that we can't go to Tofino?" he said after a few seconds. He peered at me as if I would answer. His eyes looked like a dog's that's just been kicked.

We couldn't carry Benny down. He was too heavy. So we decided we'd have to leave him there and drive back into Revelstoke to tell the police and let them figure out a way of dealing with this. Nobody said much as we walked back. The wind began to pick up and the sky clouded over. The trees crowded in on us, dark and sullen, all their magic and beckoning leaked away down a drain somewhere. The shale under our feet was loose and made going downhill much harder than uphill had been. Our feet kept slipping and we had to brace at almost every step against the possibility of their flying out from under us. The creek sang and laughed, hurried on ahead as if it had news to tell. At one point, where the stream became a waterfall, the mountain soared up straight and impassable and we had to climb right in close along the edge of the current. You couldn't tell how far the water fell. Only that it lost itself in a tangle of turns and trees. If we could get past this spot we'd be okay.

FISHING MEN

I was reading the paper after my first day back at work and finally found the article I'd been looking for. So, it was a father and son. The father drowning when we got to them and the son already dead, caught up under the boat somehow. Or maybe not. Maybe not dead yet but realizing in the last seconds before he blacked out, before hope didn't matter anymore, that if someone was rescuing them he'd never get to him down there. That it was all over. Even maybe thinking about his father instead of thinking about death. Thinking it was his father's fault that the boat had tipped.

I have nightmares about that lake, even now ten years later. I'm alone, looking out over the glass-still water at an unusual time of day. Late evening when fishermen have given up and gone home, or morning when the June sun is already too high at five o'clock to colour the slate sky. The water is stainless steel. You can't see into it. The bush is thick with silent animals and fish swirl everywhere just below the surface. I spy on the lake. My eyes search it slowly from one end to the other without my head moving at all. Suddenly a hand, from the elbow up, fingers curled, is there, just at the edge of my sight where there was only water before. It doesn't emerge; there's no action, no motion; it just appears. It's as if the thing that pushes the hand up has been waiting for the right moment, for a flicker in my concentration. Its finger doesn't beckon me.

The description of the drowning was tacked on at the end of the sports pages after features on the Thompson King Miner Festival and a possible new addition to the racquetball courts in the spring. Of course you couldn't expect the *Thompson Citizen* to headline the story. Drownings are regular events in country where the lakes are forty miles long. Lakes like Paint, Setting, Partridge Crop. But to me, then, it had seemed the most significant event of my life. More forceful even than the fact that the Iranians weren't intending to give up the American hostages, the talk of the high school staff room. It bothered me for some reason that these deaths seemed to matter only to me. How can something like that incapacitate you? You go to funerals, you see it on television, there's talk in Thompson now and then of a miner crushed under tons of ore, it's common enough. But this one had got to me. I'd spent a week at home with a stomach so tight I couldn't straighten my back.

Mainly foreigners fish at Mild Lake. Portuguese and Italians and east-coasters from the Inco mine. Locals, Manitobans, haven't got trout in their blood. They're used to coarser fish, to the untouchable maria, or the jack that will grab at anything, that would clamp onto a set of false teeth tied to grocery string.

I love the place. Pretty. A mile-long dish of clear water garnished by full white poplar and white spruce in a part of the country that's mainly dwarf black spruce. And it's stocked with rainbows and splake. You have to know how to fish them. I love to go there, it is so wild and quiet. I've heard the wolves howl there a hundred yards from our boat.

My first son, Alan, was eight years old and he wanted to join Arlin, Stan, John and me who'd decided, because it was a warm weekend in June, to drive out there Saturday morning. But it just wasn't convenient for Alan to come. We argued about it Friday evening while I was packing.

"Please, Daddy," he asked for the fifth time, "let me come. I'm old enough. I won't be in the way." He pulled at the sleeve of my fishing jacket. It's a brown Inco parka that I've had with me on every fishing trip since. Someone in the company sold it to me for twenty bucks on the promise that I wouldn't tell how I got it.

"It's not that, Al. It's just you wouldn't be comfortable, okay? We're leaving at five in the morning and it's too early for you. Actually, we're getting up at four-thirty, right Mom? You'd be tired all day." I fiddled with my tackle box, which wasn't closing right. I didn't want to look at his face. Kids see through excuses. Why not tell them the truth?

"No I wouldn't! You said next time you go I could come with you. You promised! Please!" I had promised, as I have with many things. A lot of promises. Most of them broken. Because they don't seem practical when the time comes. Like the camp-out we've planned every winter for the last five years. I draw a picture for Alan and describe the scene to him. We'll buy a tent like this one. It's the kind they use up north for mineral exploration. A Robertson tent or something. It gets set up on a wooden platform with four-foot plywood walls and is nailed tight through these grummets. Here's where the door will be. And it'll have a little wood stove and chimney, with smoke drifting up like this, and we'll pile firewood all along one wall, here, for burning and to help keep the tent warm, see? That's the north side. Then once we've got it all ready for sleeping—because that's the first thing you want to do when it's maybe thirty below—we'll set up the ice-fishing rigs in the bay right there. I sketch in some comfortable pines hugging the shore. And we can just watch them from the tent window. All cozy, right? And then, I think to myself, though I don't tell him this, I'll sit back with a book and a glass (bottle) of wine while the kids go snowshoeing or build igloos, or make campfires in the snow. That dream tugs at me right now and I'm tempted to grab paper and draw the scene again, show it to Alan, hook Alan, plan the thing with him. He's still so energetic even after all the disappointments. It fills me with such yearning just watching him!

But something always came up that summer and I never did take him. How could I tell him I didn't want him to hear the swearing? That I didn't want to have to think twice about reaching for a beer? And I couldn't let him know that the guys really didn't want a kid along. Yet, once we were actually out there fishing I'd think, why not? Alan's okay. What's the sacrifice anyway, it's dull with the guys. Alan'd be a lot more fun to have around right now.

"Not this time. I'm sorry. It wouldn't work out," I said. Alan began to walk away, his sand-coloured hair thick and rumpled like the moosegrass in the brown glass gallon jug by the piano. "There'll be John and Stan and Arlin and me and there wouldn't be room. And you'd be the only kid. Look. We'll go again, soon. Really, I promise. Just you and me, okay?" I picked him up and gave him a hug. Pressed his face against his will into the oil-smelling cotton of my parka. Funny how the smell of oil stays long after the jack slime and minnow juice don't stink anymore. After a while he didn't resist, and after a minute of holding him tight he hugged back a little. He kept his face hidden, though, and didn't say anything.

Stan called around six o'clock.

"You packed?" he said, presumptuous as usual, a

Steinbach car salesman. His voice irritated me. He's so damn predictable. Never a change over the years in the way he thinks or speaks though he may think there's been.

"More or less." I didn't want to give him the satisfaction of being too punctual.

"Okay. Let's shoot some snooker tonight. We won't bother sleeping. Around three we can grab grease at Mama Rosa's and head out from there. Arrive by the time it gets light enough to see." His Bic lighter scratched and I could see him slide his Number Sevens back into his breast pocket.

"I don't know. Think we should?" I looked over toward the stove where Verna was packing me a lunch for tomorrow. Peter was practising his piano lesson in the living-room. Practising "Sir Patric Spens." Whose composition? Linda Niamoth? No, she did only modern stuff.

"Yeah, yeah, who needs sleep. Come on, Regier. Don't wimp out." He was playing me like a fish.

"If you think that, you don't know me," I said.

It wasn't wimping. It was Verna and the kids. I might smooth the edges a bit if I stuck around home for the evening. Help clean up after supper and then play five hundred or crokinole later with the kids. And it wasn't just smoothing edges. I missed them when I was gone. Felt, at the height of doing what we'd come out to do, that I was losing out on something back home. That, on the annual trip north, for instance, to Vandekerckhove or Reindeer, two days would have been just as good as four, and why didn't the others have a part of them that only pretended to be at peace out there with the guys in the bush? A part that bobbed and sank and struggled to the surface just out of reach of the lifebuoy?

We couldn't have arrived at a better moment. The sun was still down but its rising splash of orange and blue light, clotting underneath the blackness, made the bottom ridge of the sky into a stained-glass window leaded in places by the sharp, extra height of the odd white spruce. The boats smacking down on the water's gun-metal blue smoothness and the hulls rasping on gravel and rock were the only mars on the morning's lines and stillness. For a few moments we stood there, taking it in like water at the end of a run. Somewhere, across the lake, a tree cracked and slid down through the underbrush.

The provocation of Poseidon, the shift of ship's cargo, the slip of tectonic plates, began with the arrival of three fishermen in a little red rowboat.

"Oh shit! There's someone else here," I said to Stan who looked over his shoulder and then slid his beer bottle out of sight under the life-jacket on the floor.

He studied them. "Newfies," he said after a minute, disgusted.

"How do you know that?" I asked, squinting into the white light that by now glared off water like polished steel.

"I've got eyes," he said, and the way he did meant my physical short-sightedness was next of kin to ignorance.

"Are they coming here?" I asked, hoping we'd be left alone. There's nothing worse than having another boat park close by when you've finally hit on a good hole.

"Yeah, they are. Bastards! I should tell them where to get off!" Stan raised his fist but they were still too far off to see it.

He watched them for a while. "Look at them! Look!" he said. "What's the matter with those assholes? Look at that boat!" He pointed with his rod. "Those guys are snookered!"

I could see them now too. They weren't making very good headway for Newfoundlanders who you'd think would be used to sculling.

"Heyyyyy!" someone from the red rowboat called. "Hey! Youguysh . . . gotany whishkey?"

"No!" I yelled back. "We don't!"

After a pause the voice came again. "We'll trade . . . youbeerferit."

We ignored them.

"Lots of beer. For your whis . . . whishkey!" the spokesman ran on, cupping his hands to his mouth too late, after he'd finished speaking, even though by now they were no more than a couple of hundred feet away. The boat held an older man and two teenaged boys. The boys were quiet. One of them sat in the prow and one rowed. The older man sat at the back. They were all unshaven and looked as if they hadn't slept.

"Yer sure you don have any hard shuff?" he said, smiling at us, trying to win us over.

"No! Beat it. We don't need your company," Stan called, finally angry enough to be brave. The older man muttered something and the lake echoed with their laughter. A loon answered them from the distance. They steered away and wallowed off toward Shallow Bay.

We could hear them occasionally for the next hour or so as their boat zigzagged here and there. At one point, when they were still close enough for us to see them distinctly, the old man got up with one foot on each gunwale and began rocking the boat back and forth, throwing all his weight first on one side and then the other. There was laughter and protest from the boys who must have been less drunk. Fool, I thought. That water's cold. They'll be sorry if the thing tips. They'll expect us to rescue them, too.

We finally stop paying attention when they get far enough away. We fish but we're not getting much. The sun is high now, burning the cold out of the air and heating the boat seats and our jackets. We aren't thinking of fishing so much now as sleep and our lines float idly through water as still as ice. But then it's too quiet. Stan sits up and stares in the direction the boat has gone. I look too, but can't make out anything at all. Stan is still looking. He begins to reel in his line. Faster than is normal for trout. Then he stops reeling altogether.

"There's trouble!" he yells, throwing his rod into the

bottom of the canoe and grabbing a paddle. "They're . . . Forget your bloody line! Got to get out there!" He's already paddling, sweat drops like women's tears at a funeral suddenly splashing from his cheeks, eyes reaching out there for something that's too far away, that he'll never get. "They've tipped their damned boat!"

We figure out later that it has taken us about four minutes to get there. We're in a Grummund, the lightweight aircraft-aluminum model, but now it's sluggish as cement. I strain at the spruce shaft of the paddle. The black spruce ringing the bay we're heading for grow in size as slow as tomatoes on the vine. And then we're closer. Stan talks to me, urges me. "Hurry! Regier, paddle! COME ON! It's taking too long! Gonna be late! Where's the boat? Don't see the boat. You see their boat?" It's a plodding. A plowing of earth with horses. The prow of the canoe seems to stick in the water like clay. But we work, water pouring down our faces as though we've just come out of the lake.

"I see someone!" Stan shouts. "Only one, though! Hanging onto something. He's okay! They must be on shore. Must have swum. They on shore? WHERE IN HELL ARE THEY?"

THE CABLE SLIDER

It wasn't that the cable was slack because I'd snugged it up good with the car and it had taken me half a maddening day to do it. Now it sloped down nice and tight between the two trees at just the right angle for the kids to slide down. But it had been a few weeks since I'd greased the cable, so the slider would slide better, and that's where the rubber hit the road. Well, actually, if you got right down to it, the real problem was that I'd put the tree-house too high. Because of the kids. My wife wanted it at the first branch and I more or less agreed. Then at the last minute I changed my mind. The kids, who after all were the ones who would actually be using it, really wanted it higher up. Of course it'd be dangerous, but they could climb like monkeys, I said, and anyway, we worried far too much about them.

Judy wandered into sight on the other side of the picture window and I stopped writing to watch her. Lone kids mesmerize. They're completely spontaneous, free as wives when they're scolding. Irrational, almost. Symbols of what we'd like to be but have forgotten. She skipped half a dozen steps, stopped to think about her next posture, and then jumped on one foot the rest of the way to the tree. A robin. She slumped a hand up to the rope and held on there, one bare leg lifted to the bottom rung, head swivelling through the range of all her friends' empty yards. A dancer. With the free hand she grubbed her nose, studied the end of the finger, and then rambled up to the platform fifteen feet overhead. A raccoon. Yellow leaves rained down around her and settled like goose eider on the grass below. She stepped through the little doorway, reached for the slider, a two-foot length of 2½-inch plumbing through which the cable ran, and swung out into space, legs scissoring, hair whipping her face like a horse's mane in a storm. She reached up one hand to brush it away.

Autumn, rain, apocalyptic horses, and geese, all in together? This is the twentieth century, after all, and James and Eliot and Hemingway, I want to believe, didn't live for nothing. It seems a bit Ramboesque but I didn't intend that kind of intense death symbolism at all. All I wanted was a van Goghish, insane splash of yellow, the colour of sun—that colour beside the grey pattering rain which soaks into *The Bridge at Trinquetaille*. Geese? Okay, that was a real death image. "A goose walked over my grave."

I can't understand why so many people decide not to have kids. Of course, they all have their lists of good reasons. Take John and Rita Wamlachuk. He teaches at Red River, has done so for, oh, fifteen years, and she owns a Lads and Lassies shop off Portage Avenue, on Smith. They're rich. And they're tight. They run two cars, an old restored MG and a new model Ford Taurus. Their house isn't huge but it's one of those places with everything in it. His and hers bathrooms, matched copper pots and kettles sparkling on the cedar kitchen walls, three televisions, a sauna and whirlpool, you name it. Everything perfect, everything tidy. And like I said, they're tight. When we go out together, and that's not often, it's almost always me who pays for the drinks. They go out for dinner three, four times a week. Not Bonanza or Shakey's but Zorba's and Pantages, places like that—pricey.

The other day I got on the topic with John again. When Rita's there he won't touch it with a ten-foot pole. We'd dropped off the kids at the grandparents'. From where John and I were drinking daiquiris on the patio I could smell the hamburgers and onions frying inside. The wake of the River Rouge slapped at their dock.

"Things wouldn't be as neat around here if you had kids," I said. The red geraniums and silver dusty miller in the huge ceramic pot in its perfect spot on the clean cedar deck kept drawing my eye, a pretty girl in a short dress crossing and re-crossing her legs.

"I couldn't see us with kids. Messing around in my stuff. I've got so many valuables, things that just can't be disturbed. I'd be wired all the time." He sniffed, the way people do when they're feeling stubborn. "We're just not set up for it," he added, searching for something in his glass. I thought about the eighteen kids who had sat around my grandfather's table. About *The Crucible*'s Rebecca. There was *They Shoot Horses Don't They?* The nineteen-pound jack my son had lost earlier that summer when my cheap net broke.

"What about your name?" I said. "Want that to die with you?" The lapping by the river had stopped and the waves were now just long ropes trying to tie the boat to the shore.

"Not really. Never think about it," John said.

What an empty life, I thought then and as we drove toward the grandparents' to pick up the kids.

That cable pissed me off. Interruptions, interruptions. I've already screwed up three hours. How will I ever keep that blasted rope from slipping? Why don't those ungrateful buggers give me a hand at least? All they give a rip about is the end-product. Where the . . . where is my ⁸⁄₁₆th? I should just forget the whole bloody thing, some kid's going to kill himself if I don't get it tight. Oh for Pete's sake, I said finally, my anger fizzling.

When I finished, though, I was glad I'd taken the time and so was half of Altwelt. Southern Manitoba towns are no different from anywhere else when it comes to this sort of thing. Right away a chaos of kids crowded around the new toy. The Kehlers from across the back fence, the three new immigrant kids who'd arrived three weeks ago from Belize, and others from different corners of town. Spring in the giant's garden. Suddenly their imaginations blossomed and they played a whole variety of games, sometimes letting the slider glide into the furthest folds in their minds. The slider was an unseen tether that kept them in our yard.

After lunch, when I was just settling back down to what I guess you could call my real work, Judy sneaked up behind me and put her arms around my neck, gently, so as not to shake my pen. Her stomach warmed my bare back. An undeserved pleasure. Mother holding me in my dark room before I'd go to sleep as a kid.

"Dad," she said, "is it okay if the kids come back later to play Give Me a Wink?" She knew that she didn't have to ask.

"Of course, silly!" I said. "Should I come play too?"

"No, you can just write," she said, snuggling her chin down into my shoulder. Her hair smelled like soap and smoke.

I didn't feel at all like getting back to writing. I'd rather just have sat all day and watched Judy playing. No question that John didn't know what he was missing! Getting and spending, casting ingots in caves and worrying about this worldes good for which men swinck. Much rather this. Gold to aery thinness beat. More solid. More permanent.

It must have been the wind that startled Judy when she

swung out. Must have made her reach instinctively to clear the hair from her eyes. Because suddenly there she was hanging onto the too-fat slider by one hand. Oh, far too fat for that small hand. Mouth wide and soundless. Just eyes clinging to mine through the window. One swinging hand and arm pointing, stretching toward me. Crossing the distance to anchor itself around my neck. I couldn't move. Her eyes were twisted cords. They bound me. I could not move. I would be too late. She would be down. Her body would be broken. Her ankles would be broken. Her nose bleeding. Her eyes closed. I should run, run. Hold on! Hold on!

I hold on tight to the slider, and whirl up, past the tree-house, above the town, all of it collapsing, silent. A rush through thinning air and then cold and infinite space, the still roar of planets. When I look back, the world is a spider at the end of the cable.

Taking It Easy

Jamie Regier thought his father had been especially generous and he told him so just before he left his room. There'd been the treats after four, supper at the golf course, bowling for an hour before the leaguers played, and on the way home they'd dropped in at the book sale at school and his father had given him money to buy the *How to Draw Jet Planes* that was lying beside his pillow. He had thought that he would only need $2.95 like it said on the cover but it had cost $3.16 with tax and his dad hadn't argued when the amount changed. His father's back was disappearing through the door and the big square of yellow light shrunk. "Thanks, Dad," he said. "For spending all that money on us. You didn't have to." The black shape stopped and the light grew again. "I wanted to," his father said. "I love you, Jamie." He went out the door and closed it till only a slit of yellow showed. It was comforting to Jamie to know that there was lots of light in the hall outside his room. Every night that thought helped him fall asleep.

What irrelevancies we hang on to. What in the world does light have to do with comfort? The questions Jamie should be asking he's not ready for. Why should he be? He's not yet because he's eight. Actually, he'll never be ready for them. Not when he's thirty, not when he's eighty. No one ever is. All security is false security if you go by old people. My mother, for instance, much as she was nervous and inward and easily rattled when I was still at home, now at seventy-five must wake up breathless and fighting with worry about dying, about whether Thomas, her oldest, has had even one thought about her today and when was the last time he did, about why I phoned two days after her birthday again, about who she'll talk to when my father isn't there eating his porridge across the table from her in the morning, about the time she almost took that good-looking insurance salesman up on a drink in that hotel in Swift Current when the bus was stranded. It's probably only kids that ever feel secure.

The day had started with an argument between Verna and Peter. That wasn't unusual. When the radio alarm in the kitchen went off at seven Peter had already been lying there thinking since five. He had the kind of mind that woke up racing and gradually slowed down during the day until it hardly worked at all by supper-time. Verna was the opposite. Her brain slept through breakfast, stretched and yawned during the day and dressed itself in time for supper.

Bill Guest was interviewing some psychology prof from the University of Manitoba on raising kids. Television and violence. Peter talked gently. "Verna? You have any dreams?" That sometimes did the trick and got her going. "You still love me?" The blanket rose and fell, little swells of waves on the sand beach a day after the storm. "You okay?" No answers. Eventually he'd get down to the stuff that had tied his stomach in knots already a couple of hours ago but it wasn't wise to leap into those things.

"You on duty today?" he said, sliding a snippet of brown hair between his fingers and snuggling against her back just hard enough so she'd feel that he loved her without divining that he was waking her up. Duty day at the school always meant tension. And a taste of hell if it coincided with her periods.

"I wish I hadn't yelled at Judy last night," he said when she stayed quiet. She sighed and moved her buttocks away from his an inch, but she didn't turn around. There was a mole on her neck that might end up being cancer some day and on one side of her neck, under the ear where she couldn't quite hide it with a collar, a birthmark like a rose with a leaf but no stem. She had said yesterday when he and Judy were arguing that he was over-reacting. He'd known she was right but the words had just kept coming.

"You've been hard on us all too, the last few days," he said. She'd been inward recently, withdrawn, as if she harboured some secret anger or jealousy that she didn't want to share with anyone else. She'd been coming home from work tired. Would throw herself on the couch till he'd got supper ready and then eat without thanking him.

She turned. Her eyes were wrinkled and dark underneath, but there was a hard edge in them like those times he'd only come home in time for breakfast. That edge sometimes lasted a month or more, covering two periods possibly. He didn't drink like that anymore. Won't condescend to answer me, he thought. Thinks I'm too stupid and uncontrolled to deserve to be forgiven quickly.

"She's started having periods, you know," Verna said. He hadn't known. "You can't expect her to stay a little kid forever," she continued. Her lips were tight, curled down at the corners even while she spoke as if they'd been that way all night and hadn't had a chance to rearrange themselves, like old people's skin. She rolled away from him and pulled the quilt up around her ears.

The thing with Judy had caught Peter by surprise and that was why he'd been so hard on her. He'd gotten suspicious when she and the neighbour girl, Leona, who was staying for a sleepover, had offered to take the dog for a walk. Judy never volunteered to walk the dog. Once they were out the door, Verna laughed and said they were probably walking by Julian's house. He didn't see what she found so funny and wanted to follow them. Verna said no, the girls would be mortified if they found out. Something about it all had bothered him.

In the evening the kids watched *Coming to America*. Anything with Eddy Murphy should be restricted, he thought. So much swearing even he couldn't watch. F this and F that. That bath scene with those pretty maids suddenly emerging from the water and announcing that the royal penis was clean! But the kids had rented the machine for eight dollars and the movie for two so what could he do? He'd just remind them after it was over that those sorts of words were not allowed in their house. Sometime during the movie Julian phoned and wanted Judy. Why Judy? Why exactly her? Couldn't he pick some other girl? Couldn't they wait till they were, say, fifteen? Eleven just wasn't old enough. He hadn't had anything to do with girls until he was sixteen. Any guy who'd take Judy out would just have one thing on his mind because she looked sixteen.

"What do you want with her?" he asked, knowing the question sounded corny. The ivory plastic receiver smelled like perfume. There was a long silence with only the sound of gum-chewing on the other end. Later on, when he asked her about the walk she'd taken, Judy answered in monosyllables that were all questions, without taking her eyes off the television, her voice far off and drowsy, "What?" "What do you mean?" "Why I walked by his house?"

"Respect," he shouted, glaring at her. "I want respect. Don't you treat me like I'm a kid. I'm your father! You remember that!" With every point he made he took a step closer till he was standing over her, stabbing his finger at her face. His arms itched to shake her.

He would have kept at her but Verna stepped in front of him and held his eyes and told him to be quiet. He looked at her for a minute and charged out the door. He was surprised to find himself standing on the front steps because they never used that entrance. She shouldn't talk to me like that, he thought, but at the same time he was also thinking, What's the matter with you? What the hell's wrong with you? You don't want to do that to your girl. Rain sleeted down and cooled his neck.

After half an hour he felt cold and there was an aching between his shoulder-blades as if a flu were coming on but he stayed outside, standing for a while in front of the camper with its For Sale sign fading in the sun. It wasn't red now but pink and you couldn't read it from the road anymore. He went into the garage. I'll have to clean up in here this weekend, he thought. Why do I keep all this junk? I should have gotten rid of those studs last spring. They're completely bald. And two hamster cages. They hadn't had a hamster in three years. He walked around the yard. The tree-house needed painting but he'd never get to it this year.

Inside he made himself a cup of coffee. He had to be on the road by 5:30 the next day to get to work by 7:30. And to make it worse, he'd been getting up to go to the bathroom three or four times a night. He just wasn't getting enough sleep, that was for sure. No wonder he had a hard time concentrating on books and papers. Mornings and early afternoons he'd be sleepy and then wide awake just before he went to bed at night. One in ten Americans with prostate cancer, he thought, sipping his coffee. Maxwell House. He'd have to try to make it to The Second Cup.

He couldn't keep his mind on grading papers next day, so he left work early. When he got to his town he stopped at a corner store first before racing home. The kids'd be out of school in five minutes. He ripped scrap computer paper into strips and laid six of the irregular pieces on the dining-room table. Already there was someone coming.

"Wait," he yelled, digging for a Marks-a-Lot in the Tupperware vegetable crisper on the piano where they kept their pencils and pens. They were usually useless because the kids left the caps off them. "Don't come in here yet. Who's there?"

"Me and Abe," Jamie shouted.

Peter tore at the plastic around the chocolate bars pre-wrapped in groups of six for Hallowe'en and laid them out on the table. He wrote "Abe" and "Jamie" and the names of his other kids and their friends on the papers and laid them neatly in two rows under the bars. Then he called them to come and watched their faces as they approached.

Verna didn't want to go out to eat. She sat on the couch reading, with her feet tucked up under her black skirt. Her pantyhose were a Zeller's Easter-egg mauve. She held the *Maclean's* magazine up over her eyes. Peter could read the bold print from where he sat. "The World Eyes Canada's Johnson." He squinted but couldn't read the smaller type in the upper right-hand corner.

"I have to train the kids and yell at them and nag them about piano and hanging up their clothes and homework and then you do all the fun things with them," she hissed in his direction when it looked as though the kids weren't listening. "It's not fair. You can't always do that."

A cold draft blew through the picture window over the top of the couch and around his neck. He should have replaced the windows already but they'd have to wait at least six years till the mortgage was paid. Maybe it would help to caulk them with silicone. But first they'd have to be re-puttied and they weren't worth the work. He strained to bring on the cough that tickled his throat. The storms on the north side were too rotten to be taken down for cleaning and would fall apart the next time he tried it. She was right, of course, about the kids, but he couldn't help it. That was just how it worked out.

The kids hung around in the soft living-room chairs. For the most part there was silence. Verna had said no TV. The clock ticked. The one they'd got from their parents from Hawaii for Christmas. It still cuckooed though it had fallen off the nail on the wall at least three times. When the kids had been younger they'd yanked down on the winding chains till the clock fell. Most of the decorative plastic carving was broken off.

Every few minutes they whispered to Peter that they were hungry. "Okay, let's go, then," he said finally and got up without moving off. He stooped to check his shoe-laces. Verna laid the *Maclean's* neatly on the pile of magazines on the coffee table, and got up too. She held Jamie on her lap as they drove.

At the restaurant he stopped himself from complaining about the cost, and generally from being critical. He let the kids order the food they wanted and didn't object even when they asked for soft drinks. Verna stared into the menu, pretending they didn't have children. The food came. Judy shook half the bottle of ketchup onto her fries.

"Judy! What . . .!" he said, his hand around her arm at the elbow, squeezing. And then he stopped and turned to his plate with its mound of mashed potatoes and gravy on one side and the salisbury steak under a hill of mushrooms and onions on the other. Judy looked at him for a few seconds as if she should be spanked and then began scraping the ketchup off each French fry separately. She'd lift the fry between two fingers and run her fork down each of its four sides. Jamie tried to help her but she slapped his hand with her fork and he went back to the jet plane he'd drawn on the back of the paper place-mat. The names of Altwelt businesses shone through from the other side. After a while there was a pink, soggy pile beside a puddle of ketchup on Judy's plate. Outside, daylight faded as they ate. But it was one of those odd evenings when, instead of getting dark, the sky, cloudy and heavy with snow or rain, brightened, shimmered with a dull yellow light which made the trees, buildings and the practice green below the window glow as if day were dawning.

Douglas Reimer is a lecturer in English at the University of
Manitoba. He was born and raised in southern Manitoba,
and spent ten years teaching in northern Manitoba before
he moved to Winkler, where he has lived since 1983 with his
wife Martha and three children.